THEN AM I STRONG

THEN AM I
STRONG

By

FRANCENA H. ARNOLD

MOODY PRESS • CHICAGO

ISBN: 0-8024-0060-4

Printed in the United States of America

Chapter 1

THE WHIMPERING from the crib in the corner had been going on for some minutes before the girl on the cot could shake herself loose from the heavy sleep that kept pulling her back into its oblivion. She had been so tired when she went to bed that she had fallen asleep at once, and the piteous little voice that cried, "Mommy! Mommy!" in between the baby's half surrenders to sleep, was not sufficient to waken her quickly. But as the cries grew more insistent, with a shrill note of terror creeping in, she rolled over and reached an arm out to encircle the child. Still drugged with sleep she said, with love and impatience mingled in her voice, "Oh, you little 'fraid-cat! What *am* I going to do with you? Here, come over and spoil my sleep like you always do!"

She helped the little one over the side of the crib and drew her down to the cot.

"This bed's not big enough for one, yet every night you crawl in here with me. Can't you see I'm tired, honey? You never let me get one night of decent sleep. No wonder I can't work fast daytimes. Aren't you ashamed, you sweet little 'fraid-cat?"

The baby did not answer. Already she was fast asleep, snuggled contentedly against her mother's shoulder. Almost fiercely the girl held her close. She had wakened thoroughly now, and sleep would not be easy to recapture. How wonderful it would be to get one full night of sleep with no frightened baby voice to disturb her! She needed real rest at night if she were to meet the demands of the hard days at the shop. She had to hold her job. She *had* to! She was all that stood between this helpless, frightened baby and life's hardships and cruelty. She wanted *so* much to save the child from the things that had hurt and scarred her, the mother. She wanted to give her joy and love and security. She wanted to guide those little feet away from the pitfalls that lay so thickly around her. That was the reason she worked overtime at the shop. She wanted things for her baby.

More than anything else she wanted to be able to keep her in some better place than Mrs. Tuley's day nursery. She had a strong suspicion that Mrs. Tuley had been drinking last night when she stopped to pick up the baby. Did that happen regularly? Did Mrs. Tuley mistreat the nervous little one? Was that the cause of the fears that kept them both awake nights? Or were those fears the natural result of the apprehensions that had become the girl's own lot? If she left here, where could she find another place so cheap?

"Oh, you shouldn't ever have been born," she whispered in the darkness. "We planned so much for you and you'll have such a hard time. Everything has gone wrong. I'd do anything I could to keep you safe, but I get so tired! I haven't a thing to give you but my love and my body. My love won't wear out, but I'm afraid my body will. I'm a 'fraid-cat too, honey. I'm scared stiff of what might happen to you if I — oh, dear God, I don't know what to do!"

She heard the even breathing of the baby and knew that the little one slept soundly now because her fear had been vanquished by her mother's encircling arm.

"I wish I had someone to hold me tight and to watch while I sleep. I wish there were someone to make me feel as safe as she does now. I wonder if God could do that if I knew Him better. Could He help me to go back to sleep and forget all about the things that frighten me? I wish I knew how to find out more about Him."

There was a church on the corner where she changed cars every day, a church whose doors stood open always. Would it do any good to ask there? If she went in some day through that side door where she sometimes saw the janitor at work, would he take her to the minister or someone who would listen to her? If she said, "I want to know about God. I need Him and I don't know how to find Him," would they tell her about Him and introduce her to Him so that she could tell Him how tired she was? And how she got so frightened in the night that she wanted to scream out in terror and only kept quiet for fear of waking the other 'fraid-cat beside her? Would God listen and help her? She needed Him so desperately. There wasn't anybody else — not *any* person in all the world. And she was *so* tired. Some days she felt that she could not possibly keep on working, for the weariness and the pain in her side. She'd stop tomorrow at that church and ask. They couldn't hurt her for just asking.

Anyway she would find out. *Somebody* had to help take care of her frightened baby, and who was there except God?

Chapter 2

THE MATRON of the Susan Larrimore Home for Children sat at her desk filling out a long questionnaire. The minister's wife, in the chair in front of the desk was trying to quiet the sobs of the hysterical child on her lap and at the same time help the minister in answering the questions the matron asked.

"Yes, the name is JoAnne — JoAnne Mather. She is almost five. The date is on that birth certificate the mother left with us when she went to the hospital."

"No relatives, you say?"

"The mother said none."

"How long have you known her?"

The minister looked questioningly at his wife, seemed to calculate a bit, then he answered,

"About a year and a half, I think. Wasn't it just before Easter last year, Ethel? Wasn't Gracie one of the group that was baptized on Easter morning?"

"Oh, yes, I remember now. I took care of this baby then. Hush, honey girl! No one is going to hurt you."

The minister continued, "The mother came to us asking for help. She was very young, all alone in the world, and ill from work and worry. She seemed to have a desperate yearning for God, and when she heard the gospel, responded eagerly. We got her a place to board with one of our families, and she was happy. The woman loved the baby and was glad to care for her. Two weeks ago the mother became ill — I think she had not been well for a long time — and she lived only a few days.

"The child is very difficult, as you can judge by her present tantrum, and no one wants to keep her. The woman who had her is not well and cannot accept the responsibility. We have three small children in our home and my wife must not take this one, much as she would desire to. We have had her for four days and we are ready to accept defeat. She refuses to eat, she wakens in terror several times every night, and goes into hysterics at each new face."

The matron rose and went over to the chair. "Here, dear," she said softly. "Won't you come with me? We'll go out and see the other children."

She took hold of one of the little hands and tried to draw the child toward her. But instantly the cries that had begun to soften to sobs rose again to shrieks. The matron drew back in haste.

"Does she cry *all* the time?" she asked anxiously.

"No. When she becomes accustomed to a situation she will play contentedly for hours. She is timid with other children, but loves them when she becomes acquainted with them. She is unselfish and anxious to please. These spells of hysteria constitute the only problem. Night always terrifies her. Her mother never went out evenings because of that. Just now she is worse than usual because she misses her mother and can't understand her absence."

While this conversation was going on the minister's wife had taken the child to the window to watch the children at play outside. The matron turned toward the pair again saying confidently,

"I think we can manage her all right. We have all kinds here, and even the most difficult adjust happily eventually. Just leave her with me and don't worry."

She reached again for the child, and although the screams increased in intensity, she lifted the little one into her own arms and held her. The minister's wife looked yearningly at JoAnne for a minute as if she considered taking her back and adding her to her own already full nursery. But the minister drew her away, so with one last smile of would-be reassurance she went off.

The matron watched the car go down the drive, then carried the still crying child to her room where two helpers were summoned to her assistance. After an hour they had to acknowledge themselves defeated. For one so tiny and seemingly frail, JoAnne had amazing powers of endurance.

"I think we ought to call the doctor," said one of the young women sinking into a chair. "I don't think she *can* stop."

"I don't like to be defeated by a four-year-old," said the matron, "but she is in a state of hysteria that is beyond me. I wish —"

"Say, what's the matter here?" asked a new voice. "Boy, is that kid raisin' the roof! I heard the noise halfway down the block. What's the matter with her?"

"If you can answer that question, Nona, you will be

wiser than we are," answered the matron, smiling at the small girl who stood in the doorway.

"Let me have her. Why, the poor baby's scared to death!"

She put her own thin little arms about the child and, to the amazement of the women, drew her, unresisting, from the matron.

"You poor little 'fraid-cat," she soothed. "You poor scared little, sweet little 'fraid-cat!"

The sobs grew fainter, the baby arms clung to the rescuer, and Nona swayed back and forth as she hummed a lullaby. The matron gave a sigh of relief as she said,

"Will you let her sleep with you tonight, Nona? We'll begin the adjusting process tomorrow."

"Sure! We'll just cuddle together in my bed. I can handle her O.K. She's just a scared-to-death little honey."

The room at the end of the second floor hall was dark and quiet. The great tree outside shaded the window and kept out the beams of the street light on the corner. The sky was overcast with heavy clouds and even the outlines of the window were undiscernible. JoAnne had never known such blackness. In the room at Mrs. Byrd's where she and Mommy lived there was always light even when she woke up in the night. There was a light outside their window all night long, and Mommy never had to turn on the light when she had to get JoAnne a drink. Now, roused by the backfiring of a passing car, she looked for that sign. It was not there. And Mommy wasn't there either. She had been gone so long and hadn't come back. All around was this heavy blackness that pressed against her face. That blackness might hold *any-*

thing! She drew in her breath with a quivering little sound that was almost a sob. But it wasn't really crying. It was just trying not to. She had promised she would try hard not to cry while Mommy went away to be made well at the hospital. She had forgotten about that and cried hard yesterday when she came to this place. But that was because everything was so strange. She didn't know the people and she was afraid of the queer shapes and shadows in the rooms. She was beginning to wonder, too, about Mommy. Aunty Byrd had said she couldn't ever come back but JoAnne was sure she would for she had promised. But it had been a long time, and this was a *very* lonesome place to be.

The wind was rising and the branches made a harsh, rasping sound on the roof. The moon came from behind the clouds and cast weird tossing shadows on the wall. JoAnne gazed in frightened wonder at them, then as the long arms seemed to reach toward her she forgot her promise. With a little shriek of terror she cowered into the pillow. Quickly two comforting arms came around her and Nona's voice, still thick with sleep but full of tenderness, said,

"It's all right, honeybunch. Nona's right here and everything's O.K. Don't cry — it's only the wind making that noise. Sh-sh, honey! Come on, go to sleep. I'll sing and you close your eyes and just listen."

While she rocked back and forth in the bed she sang softly to a tune of her own making,

> Bye low, by low, baby bye low!
> Bye low, bye low, baby bye!

At first the nervous little hands clutched her fiercely,

but as the soothing melody ran on and on, they relaxed and JoAnne fell asleep. Nona placed her back on the pillow and settled to her own rest again.

"She's mine!" she whispered to herself. "Nobody else can manage her and I can! They won't dare take her away like they did the kitten and the bird. I'll teach her not to be so scared. She'll learn I'll take care of her."

Chapter 3

IT WAS SUNDAY AFTERNOON. Dinner was over, and JoAnne and Nona were on the "dishpan shift." Two of the older girls were washing, four of the "middlers" were doing the drying, while JoAnne trotted about putting dishes away. Nona watched her closely, and said proudly to her nearest neighbor,

"Isn't she pretty?"

"Not so very. She's too little and scrawny."

"She's not. She's just dainty."

"I call it skinny. And she looks like an owl in those glasses."

"You're jealous. She's going to be a very bee-yutiful person when she is bigger. You just wish you had that pretty hair and those brown eyes."

"Eyes are meant to see with, and JoAnne's are no good. She can't tell a cat from a dog across the yard."

"She can so, since she got her glasses. She never stumbles anymore, and she hasn't upset her milk for six months. I know so, Miss Smarty, and you're just jealous."

JoAnne was waiting at the pantry door, so Nona departed leaving her partner to hang up the towels. She marched off across the lawn with JoAnne trudging after her.

"Where we going, Nona?"

"To find a little peace and quiet."

"What do we want with *that*?"

"I want to have a talk with you all by ourselves."

"But where will you find peace and quiet?"

"How do I know? But I'll find some. You just watch me."

She led the way through the gate and down the street. JoAnne, trotting at her side, was appalled. Even twelve-year-olds like Nona weren't supposed to go so far.

"Nona! Are we running away? We're never allowed to come this way."

"Well, we are this time. I asked Mom Sperry and she said yes."

Across the street, through a vacant field, then into the woods.

"Oh-h-h! Are we going to the river?"

"Yes. Mom said we could if we would stay clear back by this tree. I promised her we would, and you'd better mind or I'll tend to you."

"I will, Nona. Honest I will. I haven't been naughty once since I was eight years old."

They sat down under the big oak and JoAnne waited expectantly. She had as yet no inkling as to the nature of the special occasion, but she knew better than to be inquisitive. Nona was provokingly slow, almost as if she did not know how to begin She looked out over the little stream for what seemed to JoAnne a long time. Then she drew a deep breath and began.

"JoAnne, you've got to be saved!"

"What?"

"You've got to be saved. You're eight years old and that's plenty old enough. I'm sure you've reached the age of recountability."

JoAnne stared at her in horrified surprise. "What does that mean?" she gasped.

Nona was nonplussed for a minute, then she replied, "It means you're old enough to know better and if you don't behave yourself and if you don't get saved you'll go to hell."

JoAnne was still skeptical. "Where did you learn all that stuff? Where did you get that big word? I don't believe it *is* a word."

"It is so! My Sunday school teacher said it. And about hell, I learned it out of the Bible my own self!"

"Well, what do I have to be saved from?"

"From hell, I said. And I guess you have to be saved from being a bad person, cause the verse said the wicked shall be cast into hell."

"I'm *not* a bad person, and I don't want to be one so I'll save myself from it."

"You can't."

"I can, too. I can make me behave."

"That won't help. You've already been bad lots of times. And God says the soul that sinneth has to die. I read that too in a little paper I took off the table at church. You can't say you *never* sinned!"

JoAnne looked distressed. The oval face, framed by the little curls that had crept out from her braids, was lifted to Nona's while the brown eyes behind the thick glasses were wide with fright. Nona noticed the signs of terror and hastened to explain.

"But you don't really have to die on account of your sins, 'cause Jesus died for you. You know that, don't you?"

"Oh, sure. There's lots of songs say that, but I didn't know —"

"That's why I'm telling you. This is just what it means. You *should* have to die, but 'cause Jesus died you don't have to, *if* you'll let Him save you."

"Oh, I *will!*"

"You've got to understand and get it straight. It's like this. We *all* have sinned. That means everybody, JoAnne, — even me."

"Yes, I know you have," agreed JoAnne. "I can remem —"

"We can't talk about that now," interrupted Nona hastily. "We have to hurry. All of us — everybody — sinned and God hates sin. Miss Pearson said so. So everybody was s'posed to die. But God didn't want them to, so he told Jesus that if He'd come down and get killed it would count for all of us. Now when folks want to get saved they tell God they're sorry and ask Him to forgive them. And He does for Jesus' sake."

"Are you saved, Nona? Did you do that?"

"Yes, I did, and I want you to. It wouldn't be worthwhile at all for me to go to heaven if you weren't there. I'd worry myself sick!"

"But I'll be there. Let me do it now, Nona. I *am* sorry, truly I am."

Under the big tree by the side of the river two little

20

girls knelt and prayed, then rose to their feet with an assurance that they had completed an important transaction.

Chapter 4

JoAnne waited in front of the school house, her eyes on the door through which the eighth graders would come. In her hand she held the white card which she had read at least twenty times since she had received it a half hour ago. "JoAnne Mather is promoted to Grade 5 A." That meant she had skipped half a grade! Now she was only three and a half years behind Nona. And Nona was four years older.

"If I can skip one more half grade I'll be just three years behind and I can be in high school one whole year while she is there. Or maybe she'll not pass. But that would be *awful!* Nona studies and studies and almost cries cause she can't get good grades. Oh, I *hope* she passes!"

Then she thought again of what Nona's passing would mean. Nona would go to high school and she would be left at Field School. Could she bear it?

"I *have* to," she whispered. "Nona can't stay behind with me. I've got to learn to walk alone. She says so!"

The door opened and a crowd of noisy girls and boys burst forth. JoAnne searched eagerly for Nona, but even through her glasses the girls looked so much alike that Nona spied her first, and left the group to join the little girl.

"Nona, did you pass?"

"Sure did!"

"Oh — oh, goody!"

"What's the matter? That first 'oh' didn't sound so happy. Didn't you want me to pass?"

"Of course I did."

"Then what's the matter?"

"Nothing."

"There is too! Didn't *you* pass?"

"Nona Malloy! You know I did!"

"Sure I do. You never do anything *but* pass, unless you skip. Did you skip, kiddie?"

"Y-yes."

"I thought so. Then what's wrong?"

"Nothing, I said."

"Come on. The truth, the whole truth, noth —"

"Well, all right then. I don't want you to go to high school while I stay at Field."

"Oh, you ninny! You can't hang on my skirt all your life. What are you afraid of?"

"I'm not afraid. I just don't like it."

"You *are* afraid. You're a 'fraid-cat!"

"I'm *not*! Nona, say I'm not!"

"Are you sure?"

" 'Course I am. Say I'm not a 'fraid-cat, Nona, please! I haven't cried at night *much* since I got to be a big girl. I wouldn't cry *any* if I could sleep in my glasses so I could see all the furniture and tell what it was. I'm not a 'fraid-cat, Nona. Please say so."

"All right — all right. Then why don't you want to stay at Field's without me? You've been going there for years and ought to know your way around.

"I do. But I feel so *hollow* without you."

"Well, it's time you learned to live your own life. Some day I might get married. Then where would you be?"

JoAnne stared at her in startled horror. "Oh, Nona, what will I ever do?" she wailed.

Nona laughed as she hugged her. "You adorable little goon! Don't you worry. I love you so much that I'd die for you and I'm not joking. I won't even get married unless my man loves you, too."

Chapter 5

JoAnne sat on the floor by the suitcase while Nona sorted piles of clothing on the bed. The dresser drawer, the middle one that had been Nona's own ever since she and JoAnne had been rooming together, was pulled out with its contents hanging over the side and spilling onto the floor. The dresser, the window sill and two chairs were covered with boxes and books and piles of miscellaneous trifles, the collection of a girl's whole lifetime.

Nona worked vigorously with zest for her task, but JoAnne sat watching her gloomily. She wished Nona wouldn't hurry so, as if she might be glad to be going away. If only she would act a little bit sorry JoAnne wouldn't feel so badly. How could she bear the thought of leaving the Home and Mom Sperry and all the girls? How could she consider leaving JoAnne behind? Why, they had slept together every night for ten years! Didn't that mean anything to Nona? At the very thought of it JoAnne bit her lip and swallowed hard. She had promised Nona last night that she'd not cry today, and so far, she had kept her word. But even though she didn't cry out loud, she was crying inside. Or maybe that funny feeling in her chest meant that her heart had broken. That must be it, for never, if she lived to be ninety years old, could she feel any worse than she did now. Hearts *did* break. She had often heard about them. Did a person die when his heart was broken, or did he just go on living with that achy lump? Which would be worse?

"Say, you!" came Nona's voice. "You look so sour you make my jaws ache. Just like one of those big pickles the Burr Oak Church sends us. Can't you give me just a teeny smile, kiddie?"

"No, I can't. I feel so — so *awful!*"

"Listen, JoAnne! You promised."

"Well, I'm not crying. I didn't promise to smile."

"It meant the same. If you're going to sit there looking like a sick kitten, I'd rather you'd howl. Go ahead and do it!"

"I don't want to."

"Go on — a nice big yowl. Get ready now. One — two —"

"I won't."

"Well, what *do* you want to do? You won't laugh, you won't cry. Could you be persuaded to lend a hand to a busy guy who has to catch the three o'clock train and has a lot of packing to do?"

"Oh, I'm sorry! What can I do? Can I pack these books and papers in this box? Are you going to take them all?"

"Sure! They're mine, and I'll need every last little scrap of a possession to give me a feeling of home in that ugly room."

28

"Is it so awfully ugly? I wish it wasn't. This room is so nice."

JoAnne looked around the room which had been their pride. Almost everything in it spoke of the hours they had spent working and playing here. The wallpaper had been faded and colorless until they had brightened it by retinting the flowers in soft, bright colors. It had taken all of their time and most of their spending money for one whole summer, but the result was delightful. The drapes and bedspread had been made from materials salvaged from "donation barrels." The bookshelves had once been two orange crates. Their construction had cost Nona a badly bruised thumb. The pictures on the walls were cut from magazines and framed in narrow strips of black gummed paper.

Outside the window, through a vista between the trees could be seen the open field, then the trees and a glimpse of the river. JoAnne had never been across the river into the country beyond. Nona used to describe all the things she could see over there. Even with her glasses on JoAnne could not see that far. It all seemed very misty and unreal to her, like a fairyland. Nona had said that some day they would get permission to go for a picnic into that wonderful place. Maybe tomorrow — then she remembered. There would not be any tomorrow for her and Nona in the Home. For today, this very day at three o'clock, Nona was leaving her!

The pile of books on the chair fell to the floor with a thump as JoAnne pushed them aside and buried her face in her arms. Her promise to Nona was forgotten as she sobbed into the old blue cushion.

"Oh, I've tried so hard but I can't 'not cry.' You're going away and you won't ever come back!"

"Why, I will, too. I'll be back next Sunday afternoon and Mom will let us take that long walk across the bridge, I'm sure."

"But you'll never come back to stay."

"No-o, I guess not. But you have only three more years in high school. Then you'll be almost seventeen and I'll be twenty-one. I'll work as hard as anything at my job and get promoted fast and I'll save my money and we'll be able to have a little apartment of our own."

"Really, Nona? Do you think we could?"

"Of course. And while I'm working in Brantwell's store you learn all you can about cooking and keeping house. I'll never be much of a cook, so you will have to get ready to help out. Can't you do that, honey?"

JoAnne drew a long breath, then said in a shaky but determined little voice,

"Yes, I can, and I will, Nona. I'll study as hard as I can, and I'll learn to cook lots of things. And I'll sew even if I do hate it. And I'll try as hard as I can not to be lonesome."

"That's my girl! Every time you feel a lonesome coming on, come up here and make some plans for our home. JoAnne, honey, we're going to have one someday — a home of our own!"

Chapter 6

In the shipping room of Brantwell's great store, JoAnne stood hesitantly before the desk. She had been down here several times, but it never failed to frighten and confuse her. As the youngest worker in the shipping office upstairs, she was the one who was called on to run all the errands. After many bewildering experiences she had at last learned her way about the acres of floor space. She liked errands up on the brightly lighted floors where customers were coming and going, and where all sorts of unbelievably lovely merchandise was displayed. She wished she could stop and look at the fine furniture, the glittering silver and glass, or the richly colored drapes and rugs.

But down in this sub-basement where there were dusky corners and where one must watch continually for the hand trucks that seemed to scurry about like rats, where all seemed confusion and disorder to her, she felt a depressing sense of fear. She was well acquainted with that feeling. Her first memory of it was a shadowy one of being unable to get away from some unknown danger, of darkness and panic and hysterics that sought comfort in some one's arms, probably her mother's. She remembered, too, nights at the Home when the furniture in the corners of the room looked like strange and fearsome animals, and when the shadows of the branches outside the window became, to her near-sighted eyes, the waving arms of some horrible creature. Then it was Nona's arms that had held her and Nona's voice that had reassured her.

She knew now that those fears were childish and unreasonable, but their memory still haunted her. She did not like to ride in the subway because of the darkness outside the car windows. She drew the shades and turned on the lights in the little apartment as soon as the sun set. And every time she had to come down to this room the old cold fear squeezed her heart and almost choked her. She was relieved when the papers were handed back to her and she could hurry back to the lighted escalator.

Just as she was ready to step on the moving stair, with the papers in one hand and her glasses, which needed cleaning, in the other, a strong arm jerked her back and a laughing voice said,

"Not so fast, miss, not so fast. *That* one leads down into depths where little girls shouldn't go. This one is yours."

"Oh, I didn't see. My glasses are —"

But she was already being carried up by the moving steps on which she had been deposited with little ceremony. It was silly to go on talking so she concentrated on wondering when she would reach the top. If only she hadn't taken off her glasses! She didn't dare try to put them on while moving, and without them she could not see the floor. But as she neared the top the same arm came out to steady her and the voice said,

"There you are! Service of the special Brantwell type!"

"Why, how did you get here? You were down there!"

"Yes'm. But I came *up* on the *down*. It can be done if your feet are clever. Mine are."

"It makes me shudder. Why did you do it?"

"To be sure you got off right side up. Why aren't those glasses on your nose where they belong?"

"I took them off to polish them. I know better than to do that when I'm walking, but I keep on doing it."

He started to the next escalator with her but she hurriedly put on her glasses.

"I'll be all right," she said in confusion. "I can get about alone, really I can."

"Well, don't try it again with just two eyes."

He stood watching her until she had passed out of his sight. Then he turned as an old man who was working on an elevator door that was stuck, spoke to him.

"Who that, Dave?"

"Nona Malloy's little sister."

"She work here?"

"Yep. Been here a couple of years, I guess. I don't know exactly."

"She too leeta to work."

"I guess she's older than she looks."

"Too leeta to work. Just a letta beeta keeda."

"Well, Nona can take care of her."

He turned to go back to the basement to attend to his own unfinished business there. The descending escalator was six feet away from him, so with a well-timed leap he landed on the ascending one, ran lightly down it and then sprinted down the long stock room. As he ran he chuckled, "Leeta beeta keeda! He's sure right!"

The man who was waiting for him greeted him sarcastically, "You're gonna pull that trick once too often, Smarty!"

"I'm not afraid. It's not hard if you keep your eyes open and your feet where they belong."

"I'm not talkin' about you gettin' hurt. I mean the boss'll catch you."

"Has he ever said it shouldn't be done?"

"No. Guess he forgot to think of it. But someday he will."

"That'll be plenty of time to quit it. In the meantime I do it to keep my feet limber."

"Your brains are in your feet."

"How right you are! But if they were in my head I'd be ambitious and would take your job away from you. As it is, I just follow where my feet lead — and we go places."

"Watch out you don't go some place you aint headin' for."

"Thanks for the advice. Just now I'm headed for the front office. When I get me a chair and desk in there you can brag about knowing me when I was a lowly errand boy."

"I'll say I knew you when you were an escalator hopper. Here's your papers. Get along with you, Dave — and I hope you don't break your neck!"

This last was called after a retreating figure, for Dave was already far down the room. He had leaped on one of the trucks as it hurried past and was now waving a hand from the top of a pile of heavy boxes. When the truck reached the escalator he dismounted with a flying leap, landed on the descending steps and ran up them three at a time. As he dashed for an open elevator nearby, he muttered, "Leeta, beeta keeda! He's sure right. *Somebody* has to take care of her."

JoAnne had often seen Dave Robertson. Like herself he seemed to be a "traveling representative," as Nona said. But JoAnne ran errands for the shipping office, and Dave transacted business for the personnel department. Obviously there was a vast difference. JoAnne carried papers to different departments, and in between trips she typed monotonously dull pages of figures and addresses, and made out shipping labels. But Dave dealt with *people,* and rumor had it that he was so successful in that line that Mr. Brantwell was thinking of making Dave his special assistant. The workers in the different departments had learned to look for the quick figure that was apt to come to a sliding stop after a sprint from the elevator, and to laugh at the nonsensical banter with which he greeted them. They had also learned that "the troubleshooter," as Nona called him, could be very businesslike when dealing with a problem. He and Nona had formed a comradely friendship which extended only to the limits of the store, but JoAnne had never spoken to him until the meeting in the basement. When she told Nona, over their supper table that night, about the rescue on the stairs, Nona laughed.

"I suppose you got in his way. He wouldn't hurt a worm, but if anything from a worm to a cow got in his way when he was going so fast he'd — "

"He'd jump over it. I've heard the girls tell of the *craziest* things he does. But it scares me to think of that escalator trick."

"Phooey! That's nothing. I could do that myself."

'Well, don't, *please*."

"I won't — for your sake. But I've always wanted to. Don't worry about Dave. He won't get hurt. He's like a cat on his feet."

"The girls in the filing department call him 'Twinkle Toes,'" giggled JoAnne.

"Wow! Wouldn't he like that? I must remember it and use it on him if he gets fresh. It was lucky for you that he was there today. How many times have I told you never to take off your glasses when you are walk-ing? You're blind as a mole without them."

"I know it, and I'm sorry. But when they get dirty it seems like there's cobwebs in my eyes and I forget."

"Well, you practice remembering or I'll be afraid to let you out of my sight."

JoAnne did remember for many weeks. In the first place, she knew that Nona was right. She was not safe without those thick glasses that drove back the shadows and brought objects into focus for her. Then too, she must not worry Nona who had been a dear big sister to her ever since she was taken, a hysterical little orphan, to the Home. Nona hadn't been well since December when she had that stubborn cold. JoAnne wished she would take a long vacation, but before she would con-sent to that she must be convinced that JoAnne was capable of caring for herself. For there wasn't money enough for two vacations. So, as she went about the store she resolutely reminded herself of her promise and waited until she was back at her desk before taking off the bothersome glasses.

She met Dave Robertson occasionally, and he always greeted her cheerily and often he would escort her to an elevator or on an escalator with an injunction to "keep your specs on, Grandma." From the girls she might have resented the teasing, but she realized that Dave's solicitude was genuine so she smiled a "thank you" and went on her way.

Her campaign of safety was greatly facilitated by a promotion. No longer did she go about the offices on errands. Instead she was in the stenographic department, learning to use a dictaphone. So all day she sat at her desk, and it was safe to take off the glasses anytime she desired. Best of all, Nona was in the same room just three desks away. Life was secure and serene.

Chapter 7

At the close of a March day JoAnne stepped out of the store into a fine mist. How glad she was that Nona had yielded to her pleadings and stayed at home today. This cold mist would have done that cough no good. In fact, JoAnne did not think it could be beneficial to *anyone*. She shivered even in her heaviest coat, and shook her head impatiently as the drops gathered on her glasses. Getting home tonight was most decidedly not going to be fun!

She crossed the first street in a crowd of pedestrians, but when she reached the next crossing there were fewer people and she feared to step out when she could not see the lights.

"I can't go on forever just following other folks," she reasoned to herself. "There are too many jaywalkers running loose. I'll just *have* to clean my glasses."

She stepped out of the traffic and in the shelter of a building took off her glasses and dried them on her handkerchief. Now she could manage the one more block to the bus stop. As she raised her hand to replace the glasses a group of clerks came surging out of the door, jostling and hurrying and pushing against each other. One minute she had the glasses in her hand, then she felt some one stumble against her and they were gone. She cried out in consternation, but the crowd shouldered past, oblivious of her distress. Even if her eyes had been keen she could not have seen anything so small in that misty gloom with hundreds of feet tramping by. Without her glasses she was utterly helpless for her vision became blurred within a few inches. She shrank further back against the building and began to fumble in her purse for the "spares" that Nona had insisted that she carry always. But even as she searched she remembered with a cold fear at her heart that she had left them at home on the dresser. She had hoped that Nona would not discover them, for that would mean a scolding. Now she realized why Nona was so strict in this matter, for here she was with no glasses, forty blocks from home and she could not see to cross the street or read the signs on the bus. She might ask a policeman to put her on the right one, but she could not tell a policeman from anyone else. She might speak to the wrong person and get into trouble. Nona was always tellling her *never* to speak to strangers.

"What will I *do*? Oh, what *will* I do?" she moaned, gazing desperately at the passing crowd. She could not have recognized even Nona in that light. The rain increased and her coat was getting soaked. She was shaking and her teeth chattered with cold and fear. "I don't know what I'll *ever* do," she whispered.

A man brushed against her, turned to apologize, then seized her arm. She drew back in fright, but felt a surge of relief as Dave Robertson's voice spoke anxiously.

"Why, it's JoAnne! What in the world are you doing here? And where are those specs?"

She clung to him, almost sobbing in her relief. "Oh, I've lost them! They fell and are gone, and I can't see to get home and Nona will be so worried, and I'm so cold and afraid!"

He turned to look for the glasses, but they had been kicked away by the hurrying feet and were by this time, no doubt, lying in the gutter in ruins. He turned again to JoAnne who was clutching his arm as if she thought he might escape her.

"Oh, I've been *so* frightened! I can't see the bus name or number in this rain, and I'm afraid to cross the street."

"I guess the glasses are a total loss, keeda. Now if you will say where to, I'll take you home."

"I can go if you'll put me on the bus — really I can. It's number 21. It stops just three doors from our apartment."

"I wouldn't trust you to take three steps. Come on, it's too wet and cold to tarry."

Thankfully she accepted his arm and let him lead her across the street. She drew a long breath as she sank into the seat of the bus.

"I'm so glad you came along. I was going to ask a policeman to help me, but I couldn't see one, and — "

"I'll say you couldn't see one!" answered Dave grimly. "And if I hadn't worked late you'd have been a gone goose."

"I know it," she answered humbly. "I'm always get-

41

ting into messes. Nona usually pulls me out, but tonight she's at home and I was really frightened. Nona will say that God sent you to take care of me."

"Maybe she's right at that. I'm beginning to suspect that it's too big a job for a mere mortal. You sure need a guardian. You ought to keep extra specs at each end of the line and carry a pair in your purse."

"I do — er — I mean I usually do. No, I *sometimes* do. Other times I forget."

Dave chuckled. "I am sure you forget. Old Tony is right. You need someone to take care of you till you can grow up."

"Oh, Nona does that. And she does it well, too."

"I'm sure she does. But it's time she had help."

JoAnne decided it was time to turn the conversation to topics less embarrassing, and for the rest of the ride she managed to avoid the discussion of her shortcomings.

When they reached the apartment the rain had become a downpour, and they stopped in the hallway to shake the drops from scarf and hat.

"Nona is going to be cross," moaned JoAnne. "I'd almost as soon stay out here as to go in and face her. You'll come in with me, won't you, Dave? Maybe I can get her to thanking you and she will forget to scold me. Well, come on. We might as well face the firing squad!"

As her key clicked in the lock an anxious Nona con-fronted them. "Where in the world — " she began. But JoAnne forestalled her inquiries.

"I lost my glasses, Nona, and Dave brought me home. It was raining so hard I couldn't see."

"And your other glasses were on your dresser. I saw them!"

"Yes. I'm sorry, Nona. Truly I am. But wasn't it lucky that Dave came along?"

"Oh, go on with you! As long as folks like Dave and me are around to take care of you, you'll never grow up."

"I'm lots better than I used to be."

"But you're still an irresponsible infant. I ought to — "

"Send her to bed without any supper," suggested Dave as he hung his dripping hat on the doorknob.

JoAnne laughed. "That's a joke. She can't do it for I am the cook!"

"I don't believe it."

"I am so! And to prove it I am going to invite you to supper."

Dave looked from her to Nona and back again. "Can you really get a meal?" he asked.

"I certainly can. I may not be able to see my way around dark storerooms and crowded crossings, but in this apartment I'm chief housekeeper, seamstress and cook. You march into the living room and let Nona entertain you and I'll prove it in thirty minutes."

When the sounds from the small kitchen proclaimed a meal in process of making, Nona turned to Dave in dismay.

"Isn't she the limit? She needs a constant watchdog to keep her out of trouble. I've been worrying ever since I found those glasses left behind."

"She's a cute little kid but, as Tony says, she's 'too leeta to work.' "

"She will soon be nineteen, and she has to work. But it's a king-size job taking care of her. I know. I've been doing it for almost fifteen years."

A spell of coughing shook her and Dave looked at her anxiously. "It sounds as if someone needed to take care of you," he said when she had become quiet.

"Oh, it's just a cold I haven't been able to throw off. I get plenty of care. JoAnne is a regular old hen when it comes to taking care of me. You can almost hear her cluck."

"I'm glad you can take care of each other. But I think you need someone more skillful than JoAnne to doctor you. Have you been to see Miss Moxon?"

"I've taken enough of her old sulfa tablets to kill anyone less tough than an Orphanage kid."

"Are you girls Orphanage kids, as you call it?"

"Yes, we are. And we're not ashamed of it, either!"

"Well, calm down; I didn't say you should be. You don't have to take my head off!"

Nona laughed. "Excuse me. I'm a bit touchy on that score, I guess. I've got so tired of hearing folks express surprise that such civilized girls as we are came from an orphanage that my skin has become a bit tender in that spot."

"Are you half-sisters, or cousins?"

"Neither — no relation at all. I can't remember when I wasn't at the Home. When I was nine and as lonesome as a kid could possibly be among forty other lonesome kids, JoAnne was brought in. We belonged to each other at once, and we have belonged ever since."

"Yes," came JoAnne's voice from the doorway. "We need each other. I need her to make me wear my glasses, to remind me to put on my galoshes and to tell me when my face needs washing. But she needs me more than that. She needs me to cook for her!"

Nona laughed shamefacedly. "There's more truth than poetry to that. I can't cook even the simplest items."

"You don't want to," corrected JoAnne. "But that's O.K. by me! I'd rather do all the cooking than try to eat your 'items.' Now if you folks can transfer your discussion to the kitchen, we'll eat. Dave will have to bring that hassock and a pillow. There isn't room for another chair in the kitchen and if there were there isn't another chair to be had."

True to her promise, JoAnne had demonstrated her ability to cook. The meal was simple but it was well prepared and to Dave, sated with restaurant food, it was a real treat. The steak which had been planned for two had to serve three, but there were potatoes in abundance, the gravy was rich and brown, and the baking powder biscuits were a triumph of feathery lightness. Nona looked at the salad appraisingly for she had thought there was nothing in the icebox that could possibly be made into a salad. She tasted it gingerly, then decided to eat it tonight and inquire tomorrow as to its component parts. Dave, reaching for his fourth biscuit with one hand and a jar of raspberry jam with the other said enviously,

"Do you girls live like this all the time?"

"No," answered Nona. "Sometimes just before pay-day we eat spaghetti and cabbage. Ugh!"

45

"If JoAnne cooked them, even spaghetti and cabbage might be good."

"Well they aren't. And please give *me* a little credit for this meal. I put these potatoes on before you ducks got home."

"Excuse me!" Dave answered contritely. "I knew there was something special about them. Now I understand. They're so — so — done!"

Dave insisted on helping JoAnne with the dishes while Nona went back to the davenport and her menthol inhaler.

"I don't like that cold of Nona's," said Dave as he gathered up the dishes and piled them on the sink. "Why doesn't she go to the doctor?"

"I wish she would, but I can't make her do it. She bosses me but I can't boss her. It's been the other way too long."

"You're quite a team, you two. But if you don't want trouble, you'd better get Doc Herman out here. Nona ought to be in bed right now."

"I know it. Maybe you can make her listen. I get *so* worried about her. I don't know what I'd do if anything happened to Nona!"

On his way home after an evening spent in the pleasant little apartment, Dave frowned in remembrance of that deep cough. Then a picture came to him of a frightened little figure shivering in the rain on a downtown corner while an unheeding crowd milled past.

"She's just a 'leeta beeta keeda.' And she sure needs someone to take care of her. What *would* she do if anything happened to Nona?"

Chapter 8

At Dave's insistence Dr. Herman went out to see Nona and immediately ordered her to bed.

"At least two weeks of complete rest. And no cheating, young lady! A cold like this is no joke and can't be fooled with."

JoAnne began, as Nona put it, to "cluck," like a worried old hen with one chick. She installed the radio at the bedside, brought books and magazines for each day's reading, asked a neighbor to come in and heat soup for lunch, and ran the household with such a high hand that Dave, coming in with a prescription he had had filled at the corner drugstore, laughed delightedly.

"She's like a kid playing house," he said standing at Nona's bedside. "She's so little and so capable that she's funny."

"Yes, she's capable in this atmosphere," Nona croaked wearily. "But she can't remember her glasses and she can't keep directions straight, and she's absolutely hysterical in the dark. I've *got* to get well right away, Dave. I can't bear for her to come home alone evenings."

"Well, I'll see to that. Don't you worry. I live only a few blocks from here and I'll see her safe inside until you can take over again. We'll call it a part of my day's work for Brantwell's."

Nona drew a breath of relief. "You're going to a lot of trouble, Dave, but I'm so tired and worried that I can't refuse. Your job has nothing to do with it. It's just another of the things you've been doing to make life easier for me ever since I came to Brantwell's. I ought not to let you do it, but I can't — "

Her voice broke and Dave picked up the sentence.

"You can't help yourself. Didn't we agree to be pals the day we met, two scared kids, in the personnel office of the store? As your pal I'm taking over the care of your infant for a few weeks, so you go to sleep and don't worry."

As he turned to go, Nona smiled with a spark of her old vivacity. "O.K. Good luck to you, baby-sitter!"

By the time the warmer days of April had come and Nona was back in the store, Dave had established himself as a permanent counselor to the girls. He had given up the pretense of doing it as a part of his duties for the store and had invented a relationship to justify his interest in them.

"Let Cousin Dave handle that," he would say of any problem that arose, and the girls, glad for this friendship that brought new zest to their lives, grew to depend on him more than they realized. To JoAnne he was teasingly familiar as an older brother might have been, yet watched over her carefully. He seemed to have caught Nona's attitude of solicitation for a younger, tenderly loved sister. Between him and Nona there was an understanding friendship that often made JoAnne wonder just how deep it was. Was Nona going to find in Dave the husband they had talked and dreamed about? The thought of such a thing should have made her happy, for surely no one could be finer for Nona than Dave. But it didn't. She never had liked change and if Nona ever married it would certainly change everything for both of them.

"But it's right she should marry," she whispered to herself. "I won't say a thing to show how badly I'd feel. I'll just try to grow up as fast as I can so they won't have to think of me."

As the summer wore on, Dave's increasing interest became noticeable to Nona's fellow workers and she had to endure much teasing which, however, did not disturb her. She only answered with a quiet smile and went on about her work which always seemed to be piled high in the basket on her desk.

"The old fingers seem to have lost their punch. I never catch up any more," she said.

"You're in love," said her neighbor at the next desk. "It makes dreamers out of the best of us."

Occasionally Dave would take the old car that he and his roommate owned, and would drive the girls out into the country for a quiet Sunday afternoon. He would leave the highways with their heavy traffic and seek out the graveled lanes where the summer weeds grew thick along the roadside and where the trees often leaned over to brush the car top.

"I love it! I love it! I *love* it!" cried JoAnne from

49

the back seat where she sat guarding the lunch basket. "I wish my eyes could look both ways at once. I'm always missing something special on my right side while I look at something super on my left."

"Well, you can smell from both sides at once," comforted Nona, drawing in long breaths of the clean air. "If I could live out here and sleep in a tent I'd feel like a new woman."

"Some day Cousin Dave will buy a farm, then marry one of you girls and move out."

JoAnne caught the flush that crept into Nona's cheeks at this remark, and the suspicions that had been in her mind crystallized into certainty.

"That would be fine," she assented smugly. "You can marry Nona and take me to live with you and do your cooking."

"He'll do nothing of the sort," said Nona with an embarrassed laugh. "I'm not going to marry until I find a man who can hire a cook!"

"Give me a few more years, woman, and I'll hire you two cooks if you want them. Two cooks and a nurse-girl to take care of JoAnne."

"O.K. It's a deal," said Nona laughingly. But JoAnne retired huffily behind the pages of the magazine she had brought along.

On one summer night when the air was stifling, and the night bade fair to be a sleepless one, Dave suggested that he call for them in the morning in time to go to the beach and see the sun rise over the lake.

"Sunrise!" exclaimed Nona. "What time does the sun rise in July?"

"Oh, about five o'clock."

"Nothing doing! I'm not going to get out of bed at *that* hour to see a sunrise. It will have to get up without my help."

"Aw, come on! It will be refreshing after such a hot night."

"These nights aren't hot. They're just comfortable. I'd freeze to death out there on the lake front at dawn."

"Well, you can stay here and keep warm," said Dave soberly. "Perhaps it wouldn't be best. It *is* a little cool out there at five o'clock. We don't want you to take cold again. But JoAnne and I can go. What say, Four-eyes?"

"I'd love to! I haven't seen a sunrise since we came to the city."

Dawn on the lake shore was a sight JoAnne never forgot. It was just beginning to get light in the east when Dave stopped the car at the edge of the beach and they looked across the water to the first faint lifting of the pall of night. Between them and the horizon the water looked dark and cold with a gray mist rising over it. For a moment a cold sense of depression and fear held JoAnne.

"The water is cold and gruesome, isn't it? It's so *dark*."

"I didn't bring you out here to show you the water. Look up at the sky, JoAnne!"

She looked and drew in a breath of awe. In the few minutes that her eyes had been lowered to the water the skyline had lightened and the promise of a radiant morn was flung across the heavens. She reached for

Dave's hand and held it tightly as they stood together watching in speechless joy the miracle of a new day. The early morning breeze lifted their hair and brought an infilling of vigor and freshness that swept away the weariness of the sultry night. As the sun climbed from behind the horizon the water, which had been dark and forbidding, became bright with a shining path across it, a path that led directly from the sun to their feet.

JoAnne whispered in delight, "Oh, I love the sunrise! It's so hopeful. It gets brighter and brighter all the time!"

"And in an hour or so it will be so hot that we'll be scorching. Let's have a run along the beach before we have to go hunt some breakfast."

Hand-in-hand they raced along the sand. JoAnne was small, but she was light and fleet, and Dave had no trouble suiting his pace to her's. As they stood at last by the car ready to start back to the busyness of the day she said, as she smoothed her hair.

"It's been such a treat, Dave. I wish Nona could have come with us."

"So do I. But Nona isn't quite up to such hoydenish tricks. You'll have to take care of her, JoAnne. She's a pretty precious package, and she doesn't have the pep she should."

"I know it. She used to *never* be tired, and now she's tired all the time."

"We'll have to see that she gets plenty of rest. But while she is resting you and I will come out occasionally to greet a sunrise. O.K.?"

"O.K. As I remarked before, I love sunrises!"

Chapter 9

W<small>HEN</small> N<small>ONA</small> <small>HAD</small> <small>COME</small> to the city alone she had not attended any church, for every Sunday had been spent at the Home with JoAnne. She had attended church with "the family" from the orphanage and had been happy to have the feeling of still belonging. Mom Sperry's motherly heart followed all her boys and girls when they went out into the world, and whenever any of them could return they were received with open arms.

But shortly after JoAnne had joined Nona in the city, Mom Sperry had resigned and gone to California to live with a sister, and a new matron had been appointed, "one that knew not Joseph," an assistant had asserted grimly. The Home was no longer a sanctuary to which the girls could retire for comfort or encouragement, and they had ceased their visits.

For a number of weeks they had visited churches in their neighborhood, and had finally settled on Grace Church, just a few blocks from their apartment, as the one they would join. The middle-aged pastor and his wife were interested and kindly, the young people busy and friendly, and best of all Nona said, "The sermons come from the Bible." This had not been the case in some of the churches visited, and Nona had quickly scratched them off her list.

"We've got no time to waste on that church," she said firmly when JoAnne had been attracted by the beautiful music and eloquent oratory they found in one magnificent Gothic cathedral. "There's too much form and ceremony."

"But that's no sign they aren't sincere or right," argued JoAnne. "They might just like to do things in that nice dignified way. I enjoyed it."

"Well, if they enjoy it, let them have it. Maybe their beliefs *are* all right. I hope so. But none of that for me. All that rigamarole makes too heavy a smoke screen between me and God."

"I didn't feel that way at all. It gave me a sort of worshipful feeling."

"You can go there, then. I couldn't. I'm just Nona Malloy from an orphanage, and I've got sense enough to know where I don't belong. You go there and I'll find me a pint-size church with no trimmings."

"You know I wouldn't go without you. I guess there was a little too much formality in that church. I wouldn't like a steady diet of it. But I didn't care for that church we went to last week either. I didn't fit in there. Everything was noisy. The preacher yelled, the pianist pounded like crazy, and the soloist had the 'blues.' "

Nona laughed. "We'll compromise. We'll try to find a place that's dignified enough for you and not too stiff for me. Let's go to Grace again next Sunday. We both like that. It's like the church out home."

So to Grace Church they went, and found there training, inspiration and fellowship. On Sunday evenings Dave went with them. But although he seemed to feel a lively interest in the youth meetings he avoided any active part in them beyond joining in the singing. Nona watched him closely during the invitations that always came at the close of the sermons, but his attitude implied that these did not concern him.

One night in October as the girls were eating their supper Nona spoke soberly,

"JoAnne do you think Dave is a Christian?"

JoAnne looked startled. "I don't know. I suppose he is. I never thought that he might not be. What makes you ask?"

Nona's flush showed her confusion at this question. "He's our friend, isn't he? We ought to know whether our friends are Christians. If they aren't we ought to do all that we can to help them become Christians."

JoAnne's lips twitched at a sudden memory that assailed her. "How? Take them down by the river and scare them into it?"

Nona laughed with her as the picture of that long ago Sunday afternoon came back.

"My methods were pretty drastic, I guess, but they were effective. At least, I hope they were. You are a truly born again Christian aren't you, honey?"

JoAnne's face sobered. "Of course I am. You can rest assured, Nona, that I *know* I'm saved. I've never had a minute's doubt of that. I meant it when I accepted

Christ that day. If you and I are different in some ways we are together in that. But what stirred you up about Dave? He's such a grand fellow. I'm sure he's all right."

"Being a grand fellow doesn't mean being a Christian. Going to church doesn't mean it, either. I've got to know for sure."

JoAnne said nothing, for her own thoughts were busy with an idea that had just come and which made her feel unaccountably depressed. She said nothing, but thought,

"She knows she shouldn't marry anyone who isn't a Christian. I wonder if he has asked her."

The next evening that Dave came over JoAnne called some of the girls from the church and asked them to come past on their way to a meeting at the church.

"I'd better be finding other interests and friends," she reasoned to herself. "I'm not going to hang around in Nona's and Dave's way if I can help it. Nona has to have her chance. I've been hanging around her neck too long. Some day I guess I'll get *my* chance too. I know there isn't another man in the world as nice as Dave, but I'll make me be satisfied with the second-best one." She ran the comb through her hair as she stood in front of her mirror, then gave back a smile at the girl therein. "Good luck, Miss Mather! And watch out, Mr. Second-best. Here I come!"

She waved an airy good-by to Dave and Nona and promised to be back at ten o'clock. Dave watched her go with puzzled surprise, then turned to Nona questioningly.

"What's the idea? Doesn't she like our company?

Have I been making a pest of myself barging in here so often?"

"I don't know. And tonight I don't care. I want to talk to you about something special, and even JoAnne might be in the way."

"What's up? Am I on the carpet? Have I been out of bounds?"

"No, of course not. I just wondered — I can't be sure by your actions — a person doesn't know — oh, I can't say it any way except right out! Dave, are you a Christian?"

He stared at her in astonishment, then answered shortly, "Of course I am."

"Please don't be angry, Dave. I don't know how to do this nicely or even politely. But I *have* to know. What do you mean by saying that you are a Christian? I've met so many folks since I came to the city that don't mean what I mean when I speak of being a Christian. Are you a really born-again one, Dave?"

Dave sensed the desperate earnestness of Nona's questioning, and did not quibble, but answered soberly,

"I know what you mean. I ought to. My folks were that kind of Christians. My dad died when I was ten but we had one talk I'll never forget. It was just the day before he died and he probably knew he was going. He put it up to me so straight I could not fail to understand. I accepted Christ that day, and it made him and mother pretty happy. As long as she lived — until just before I came here — mother and I had a good time together. She was sick over two years, and life was tough, but she — " Dave's voice faltered. "She loved

57

the Lord so much that she made it seem all right to suffer excruciating pain if it were His will."

He stopped for a moment as if he could not go on. Nona was silent, not knowing just what to say. Probably this was the first time since coming to the city that he had spoken to anyone about his mother.

"I guess I haven't worked at it very hard since then," he finally said. "I've not forgotten all I was taught. I've lived cleanly and honestly and worked like a Turk at Brantwell's and in night school. I've been pretty careless about church attendance, however. Sunday mornings I like to sleep. These evenings I've gone with you girls constitute my record for the last four years. But — to answer you directly — I am a Christian. I *know* I am. Now you answer a question. What's it all about?"

The eyes she raised to his were full of tears and her lips were trembling.

"Thank you for all you've said, Dave. You've made me very happy. It means a lot to me and has cleared up some of my thinking. You'll understand the reason for my urgency later. Just now I am feeling very much ashamed that I waited so long to ask that question of the dearest friend I ever had."

"Am I that?"

"Yes, you are. The dearest one I ever expect to have. God sent you to JoAnne and me for a very special purpose. Some day soon He may reveal it. Now you get to work on that big book you had when you came in, and I'll knit a row or two on this sweater of JoAnne's. I want her to find us as usual when she comes in."

Dave did as she said, and when ten o'clock came

JoAnne found Nona asleep on the davenport while Dave was deep in a ponderous volume on personnel problems. She threw her scarf on the table and sank into a chair, saying sarcastically,

"This is a very romantic scene. Hero studying, heroine asleep from sheer boredom."

"Fresh child!" retorted Dave, closing his book and preparing to leave. "This isn't romance. It's love of a kind a guy doesn't meet often. I'll tell you about it five years from now when you are old enough to understand."

Chapter 10

DAVE WAS HURRYING through the stenographic department the next day when Nona motioned to him. As he stopped by her desk he noticed that she looked more pale and tired than usual, and that her hand, resting on the keyboard of her machine, was trembling. Dave spoke quietly, so that even the girl at the nearest desk did not hear him.

"What's the matter, pal? Something troubling you?"

"Yes. I must see you alone, Dave. Can we go riding tonight so we can have a talk?"

"Without JoAnne?"

"Yes. I'll fix it with her."

"O.K. then. Seven-thirty? I want to get you home so you can be in bed early."

"Seven-thirty, it is. You'll understand after I've talked to you."

Dave did understand more than Nona realized, for after they had driven out a busy boulevard to the quiet country lane where they could talk quietly, he spoke soberly.

"Is it those X-rays, Nona?"

"Yes. How did you find out?"

"After I left you this afternoon I went down and talked to Miss Moxon. She told me about them — and showed them to me."

"I'm glad you know. Pretty bad, aren't they?"

"So bad that I went up and talked to Dad Brantwell. The wheels are already in motion and you are leaving for Arizona as soon as we can get a place fixed up for you."

"That's all right. Arizona is as good a place as any. I'm glad it's far enough away that JoAnne can't be coming to see me. She's been with me too much already. I'm afraid she has been infected. But, Dave, *how* can I go and leave her?"

"You *have* to go."

"I know it. Any way I look at it I have to leave her. I am thinking a lot these days about how her mother must have felt fifteen years ago when she had to go." She spoke hurriedly as if she feared she might not be able to say all that lay on her heart. "If I go to Arizona she will be left here alone. And if I don't go she will soon be alone anyway. Dr. Herman says it will be less than a year if I try to stay here. And I'd be endangering JoAnne if I stay with her. So in any case JoAnne will be left alone."

"Not all alone, Nona. I'll be here."

"I want to tell you about her," she went on, unheeding his remark. "I know you think I treat her like a baby. But you do the same. There's just something about her—"

"Definitely."

"I can't tell you how I feel about her, Dave. She is

all the family I ever had. I probably came from pretty poor stuff. Once a boy at school called me an alley cat. I guess he wasn't far wrong. I was left in an 'L' station in a basket when I was about a week old. I'm not even sure of my name and birthday, or of my nationality. I always thought they took us by turn. It was my turn to be Irish, so Malloy I became. But JoAnne is different. She is quality. I don't know why her mother was all alone when she died and left JoAnne to be put in the Home. But I do know that JoAnne is a real lady. And she's mine! I raised her and trained her. I led her to the Lord, and I've tried to teach her to trust in Him for everything. I don't think she has gone very far in that direction yet because she trusts in me instead. But she's so young. Life will have to teach her the things I couldn't. I've taught her all she knows — except in cooking," she finished with a short laugh.

She went on swiftly, as if she feared her emotions. "But now I have to leave her Dave. For her sake I have to go quickly."

"You're pretty high quality yourself," said Dave huskily. "And if JoAnne is a lady it's because she was trained by the finest one I know."

"Thanks, pal. I'll remember that all my life. But to get back to JoAnne. You probably have thought that I pamper her too much. Maybe I do. But you have never seen her in a spell of hysteria so great that she almost chokes to death. That's what I've been fighting for fifteen years. Sometimes I have thought I had conquered, then some shock will bring it back. It's awful, Dave."

"But why? There must be a reason."

"There probably is, but it's hidden in the mists of antiquity. JoAnne can't remember it. I've puzzled over it many a night after she was asleep. Did someone mistreat her terribly when she was a baby? Or was it all because of her near-sighted eyes? Before she got her first glasses she could not see across a room. She used to spill her milk at every meal. Was that what made her so fearful? I've tried to brace her up to develop a little common sense and backbone. But I've been too soft where she is concerned. I couldn't do it and now it's too late. I have to leave her and she can't walk alone!"

Nona's voice broke and she struggled with the lump that hindered her speech. Dave sat in miserable silence, wanting to comfort her but not able to think of anything adequate for the situation. Then she spoke again.

"You'll have to take over, Dave."

"What do you mean? Of course, I'll do what I can."

"Let me get to the point before I — I — well, I've about reached my limit. Now you'll see why I was so urgent last night. If you weren't a Christian even you wouldn't do. Dave, will you marry JoAnne before I go?"

Dave sat in shocked silence. Then his words came explosively. "You can't mean that Nona! Of course I love her. I've loved her for months and you've known it. And I've hoped that when she is older — when she grows up more — you know — she's such a kid now — oh, I don't know what to say. It wouldn't be fair to her, Nona. She doesn't love me and we couldn't rush her into such a thing. Maybe — "

"She does love you, Dave. And she's more mature

than you think. These last months since I've been ill have changed her. She's not a child any more, even if she is afraid of the dark."

"But she doesn't love me like *that!*"

"I think she does. Last night she thought you and I were planning our marriage. She has been thinking all summer that you were courting me. And she's been so dear about it! But after you had gone last night and she thought I was asleep she was crying. It was hard not to go to her and tell her that she was the one you loved. But I didn't dare say anything. It's for you to tell her, Dave. I've known since last spring how you feel, and now I'm sure about her. I could feel so much better about leaving her if you had the right to take care of her. Will you do it, Dave?"

Dave did not answer at once. He bent his head over his hands which were gripping the wheel and sat quietly. Nona wondered if he were praying. She herself had prayed many nights over the problem. She thought this solution was of God, and waited patiently. Traffic roared past on the highway a few rods away, but they had driven off the road, and sat in the shadow of a large tree. The minutes ticked past and Nona felt cold and weary. At last Dave lifted his head and spoke haltingly.

"It all depends on JoAnne. I've dreamed a lot since last spring and have built a lot of aircastles. I thought I'd have to wait several years yet. But if you're right and JoAnne loves me — well, I'd think heaven had dropped right down on me."

Nona could hold back the tears no longer. Burying her face on Dave's shoulder she cried unrestrainedly.

He sat quietly, patting the hand that lay on his arm and waiting for the storm to pass.

"Oh, that's like a mountain off my shoulders," she said quaveringly. "It's my fault she's so helpless, but she's such a darling, and she's been all I had. I've been so worried that I couldn't sleep. Now I feel like Simeon when he told the Lord he was ready to depart in peace. I have accomplished my task."

"I'll take care of her, don't you fear," said Dave huskily. "Until I get used to the idea I'll feel like I'd stolen the crown jewels or something. But you don't have to worry. I'll be on the job."

"Thank you. And don't tell her about me until you've settled things about yourselves. She'll take it better that way."

So it came about that after they had returned to the apartment and Nona had retired to her room, Dave sat down beside JoAnne and possessing himself of the restless little hands that were busy with some knitting, told her of his love, the love that had begun on a stormy night in March and had been growing ever since. JoAnne gazed at him in amazement that had in it a hint of fright

"Dave! You don't mean that, do you? I thought that you and Nona — "

"I do love Nona, JoAnne, just like I might have loved a sister. She knows how I feel about her. We're pals. But that's not how I love you."

"But — but how — "

"How? Well, I guess it's like any man loves the woman he thinks God made for him, the woman he needs to complete his own life, the woman with whom he hopes to build a home and a family and to work through his strong years, and then journey on down the last hill together. That's as near as I can say it, darling. That's how I feel about you."

Her eyes were shining and her cheeks flushed, but she could not yet accept the love he offered. She must first be absolutely sure that love did not belong to Nona. If Nona loved Dave she should have him.

"Nona knows all about us, and she sends her blessing," he said smiling down into her eyes. "She wants this almost as much as I do. I've already told you how I feel. So the only person left to be won over is JoAnne Mather. Do you think she could be convinced that I love her and need her, and intend to have her?"

"I think she could — in fact, I *know*. Oh, Dave, you can't have failed to see! I've loved you for months. But I thought you didn't consider me anything but Nona's baby sister."

"Ever since last spring I've known you were the girl I was waiting for, and tonight I had to tell you so."

So when, a week later, Nona told her that the plans were completed and that she was to leave in ten days, it was a JoAnne held in the shelter of Dave's arms who received the shock. Although at first she was hysterically unbelieving, she grew quiet as she realized the grave import of the doctor's orders and recognized that obedience to them was Nona's only chance for life.

From that day, with no further display of emotion, they busied themselves preparing for JoAnne's wedding and Nona's departure. Mr. Brantwell was, to the world, an eccentric old-fashioned man who, because of his wealth, was able to get away with unbusinesslike methods that would have ruined a less solidly established institution than the great store that bore his name. To him his employees were his children. Their interests and their troubles were his. So Nona found herself the object of his care, and for the first time since she left the Home, she knew what it meant to lean on a stronger arm. That arm had reached to Arizona and prepared a room where she could rest and, they assured her, grow strong again.

One gray afternoon in early November with only Nona and Mr. Brantwell and his chauffeur as witnesses, JoAnne and Dave stood at the altar and spoke the vows that bound them together "until death do you part." If Nona swayed and almost fell as the solemn words, "I now pronounce you man and wife," were spoken, no one knew it except Mr. Brantwell whose arm upheld her. The other two were looking into each other's eyes and beginning to realize just how final and serious was the step they were taking. As the service ended Dave put his arms about his bride and whispered for her ear alone,

"It's forever, JoAnne."

And with her head against his shoulder she answered, "Yes, forever."

Then in the long black car that the young people had often seen but never expected to ride in they were driven downtown where, in a small dining room of a great hotel they were served such a meal in such a setting as had not entered their wildest dreams. It was all so beautiful and unusual to them that Nona's cheeks were flushed to match the pink roses in her corsage. JoAnne in her new green suit, with a white orchid on her shoulder, appeared to Mr. Brantwell's delighted eyes like one of the dolls from the toy department come to life.

But it was a white-faced girl who bit back her sobs as she told Nona good-by in the station while Dave and Mr. Brantwell stood aside, their own eyes misty as they watched.

"Good-by, little sister," said Nona briskly. "Be a good girl and take care of Dave. Write to me often and tell me all of the news from yourself and the store. And I'll be coming back before you know it. God bless you, honey!"

She turned away to Dave who helped her into the train, and although they watched eagerly she did not look back. Until the train had left the trainshed she kept her eyes on the newspaper in her hand. Then she turned to the window and watched the lights as they passed, trying to recognize, through the darkness, anything that might be familiar. Later she lay in her berth and wept for the love and life that she knew could never be hers.

JoAnne rode home sitting between the two men but hearing nothing of their conversation. At the curb before their building she thanked Mr. Brantwell and when he had gone, climbed the stairs with Dave's arm about her. As she opened her purse to look for her key Dave took one from his pocket, saying with a smile,

"Nona gave me this. It's my home, too, now." With which he lifted her over the threshold.

"Welcome home, Mrs. Robertson."

She brightened at that and answered quickly, "As soon as I can take off this orchid I am going to hug you, Dave. You're such a dear."

But when she went into the kitchen to get a vase the blackboard which the girls had used for lists and reminders to each other, greeted her with the injunction, scribbled in Nona's angular writing,

"Don't forget to pay the milk bill. The money is behind the catsup bottle. P.S. *Please* don't forget to water my violets."

That was too vivid a reminder of all the months they had spent here together. Remembrance of what Nona had meant to her through the years since she had been carried, a screaming bundle of fright, into the Home, swept over her. Nona's arms had shielded and comforted her then and it was Nona she wanted now. She forgot the vase, forgot Dave who was waiting in the hallway, and rushed into the dark living room. There she flung herself down on the davenport where Nona had lain so many evenings, and burst into sobs.

There Dave found her, and lifting her in his arms he carried her over to the big chair by the window. He made no attempt to still the crying but quietly held her close and let her feel his tender care about her. At last she spoke brokenly.

"Oh, Dave, she was all I ever had! She did *everything* for me. I couldn't have lived without her. Oh, how can I bear it?"

The tears started again and he held her more closely. After a long time she grew quiet and lay looking out at the cars as they streamed past on the boulevard. Then Dave spoke softly,

"If I turn on the lights would you like to go bathe your eyes so that you can read a letter Nona left for you?"

"A letter! Oh, yes!"

In that letter was all that Nona had not dared to try to say face to face, — her pain at leaving, her love for JoAnne, her assurance that God had sent Dave and his love at just the time they were needed.

"I knew months ago that he loved you, dear, but you are such an innocent you never caught on. He will be good for you, JoAnne, for he can do so much for you that I could not. And you will be a good wife for him. (You're a better cook than typist any day!) And someday I hope you will be the kind of mother that you and I used to talk about.

"Don't grieve for me, honey, I'll be resting and getting well in the Arizona sunshine. And you must go on to the bigger things life has for you. Don't quite forget me, though. I'll be thinking of you and praying for you every day.

"Your big sis, Nona.

"P.S. For Dave's sake, honey, *do* try to grow up!"

That last sentence, so like the Nona of the Home, brought a laugh that drove away the tears that might have come again. Dave also, had been reading a letter, and said now, with a ring of excitement in his voice,

"Listen to this! It's from Dad Brantwell. I knew he'd give me a raise. He always does when a guy gets married. But what do you know about this? Here are two reservations for a plane for Texas tomorrow, and he has telephoned the superintendent of his ranch to meet us and take care of us for a week. JoAnne Robertson, start packing your kitbag. We're going out to see some real sunrises!"

Then he grabbed her and held her close. "With a boss like Dad, and a wife like you, — what more could a guy ask of heaven?"

Chapter 11

DAVE HAD FELT that he must ask JoAnne to resign from her position at the store, but Nona had advised against it.

"Not so many changes all at once, Dave. She shouldn't be at home alone during these coming months. Let that come later."

So when they returned from Texas they went back to the office together. It was a hilarious group that greeted them, for the wedding had been a surprise to all. In the excitement JoAnne hardly noticed that the office furniture had been shifted so that the new girl was not sitting where Nona had been. There were many new experiences to carry her through the first days. Her own office group gave a linen shower for her. Dave's friends appeared at the apartment one evening with loaded arms, demanding refreshments in exchange for their gifts. The young people from the church came bearing good wishes and an array of kitchen equipment. With the stimulus of these happenings the first few weeks passed easily, and life settled down to a quiet routine.

Because of the memory which he could never lose,

ot that March evening when she had been helplessly lost on a downtown corner, Dave never let JoAnne travel alone. Together they went to and from work and together they shopped at the neighborhood stores.

This constant companionship was a great source of comfort to her. In the months since Nona had been ill she had often wondered what she would do if Nona should ever be taken from her. She had lain awake at night building all sorts of dreadful pictures of the things that could happen should she be left to her own resources. Although she had been working in the city over two years she had never overcome her terror of the downtown streets. The jostling crowds, the hurried crossings, the ever present sense of something beyond her short-sighted vision that might at any moment overwhelm her, all these became nightmares to her. Even when Nona was with her she had a feeling that some unknown threat hovered between the towering buildings on the streets where the sun was never visible at the morning and evening hours when she traveled them.

That feeling was the thing that she had feared all her life. She often tried to remember where it had come from. It was so vague that she could not describe it even to Nona. It had something to do with darkness and closing walls and sounds of strange creatures running about her. If only she could remember it clearly! But it sulked there in the back of her mind and she could never quite coax it out into the open where she could see and, perhaps, conquer it. For in spite of the teasing Nona gave her she didn't enjoy being considered a baby. And she did try to overcome her weakness. But the darkness and the wail of the wind and the gloom of heavy shadows always overcame her resistance. Where she had determined to be brave and strong she became a hysterical weakling again.

But with Dave at her side she did not notice the shadows, and with his hand on her arm she crossed the streets without realizing it. *Nothing* could happen to Dave! And Dave would let nothing happen to her.

Little by little the pucker between her eyebrows, that had shown the tenseness of her nerves, disappeared, and her face grew plump and rosy. Dave rejoiced at her blossoming and was convinced that under his care the hysterics and fears had been banished. His task was to keep her so happy that they would not return.

"Do you want to buy some new furniture?" he asked one evening as he watched her mending a slipcover. "Aren't all brides supposed to have new stuff in their homes?"

She looked up, startled.

"Could we? I thought that this all happened so suddenly — you weren't planning on getting married, I'm sure, until you found out about Nona. Oh no," as he started to interrupt. "I'm not doubting your love. That's the thing in all the world I'm surest of. But I've always thought you and Nona planned it all that night you went riding and left me at home. Now, didn't you?"

"Well, yes," he admitted a bit sheepishly. "But I'd have got round to it eventually."

"I believe that, too. But the point is, I thought you didn't have money for furniture and things."

"I don't have much money. I still owe quite a lot on

the bills when mother was sick. And I've been going to night school at the university ever since I came to the city. But there's *some* money and if you want some furniture it can be managed somehow."

"I don't think I want anything that has to be 'managed somehow.' Don't you think the apartment looks all right, Dave? Or is it all wrong? Nona and I never lived in a regular home and we didn't know much about how to fix it. And we didn't have much money. Is it wrong?"

"So far as I'm concerned it's absolutely right. That night last March when you and I came in out of the cold and rain to the light and warmth and beauty of this room, I felt like I had found a home for the first time in over four years."

"So you married me for the apartment?"

"Well — not exactly. But I'm glad it was thrown in. It may not have cost much, but it looks like a million. One of the gals who made it was an artist, — and I don't think it was Nona."

JoAnne laughed. "No, she wasn't the artist. She was the carpenter and the electrician and the plumber. She cut off the head of the bed after I got the idea. Then we made a head out of the foot and covered it with quilted satin. I think it's lovely. She made that lamp out of an old brown vinegar jug I found in a secondhand store. She built that corner cupboard in the kitchen. And she — oh, Dave, I miss her so!"

Dave took the sewing from her hands and drew her to his side.

"I know you do, chicken. But she's being cared for

better than we could ever manage here. She says she is feeling much better. She's working down there to get well, and we have a job to do here. I promised her I would do my best to make a 'growed-up woman' of you. My job is to take care of you and yours is to grow up. So — leeta, beeta keeda, start your growing!"

Winter evenings when Dave studied and JoAnne sewed or wrote long letters to Nona were times of quiet but deep happiness. When the lesson was finished the sewing would be laid aside and they would read together, both heads bent over the same book. Noting how closely she held the book, Dave grew concerned. One evening he sat watching her as she darned. He arose, went into the bedroom, and returned with two socks in his hand.

"Will you look at this pair of socks?" he said to her. "Do you see anything wrong with them?"

She examined them carefully, turning them this way and that, then looked up with a puzzled frown.

"No, I don't. What is it? Are the darns bad? I don't like to sew on black, but Nona said my darns were nice."

"The darns are O.K. Quite artistic, in fact. But honestly, JoAnne, can't you tell that one of them is blue and one black?"

Her face flushed. "No, I can't. They look the same to me."

"That's what I was afraid of. I couldn't believe that you served me assorted socks on purpose."

"Did I really mix them?"

"You really did. And it's not the first time. What do

77

you think I'm going to do about it? I'm getting tired of the razzing at the office."

"That's easy. Buy socks of different patterns. Get some checks or polka dots for a change, instead of these dark blues and blacks that *nobody* can tell apart."

"I may do that. At Christmas time I saw some in the men's department that would be fine. Bright red with black reindeer on them. But in the meantime we are going to see if anything can be done about those eyes. When were they examined last?"

"About four years ago, I think. They can't be helped."

"Who says so?"

"The doctor. He says they won't get worse, but they'll never be better."

"Maybe I'll believe that when I've heard it from a dozen of the best specialists in the city. Until then we're going to keep on trying to help them. We're going to ask Dr. Herman tomorrow to recommend someone. Everyone should have his eyes examined at regular intervals and you're no exception."

Dr. Herman was glad to recommend a friend in his own building which was in the same block as the store. Three days a week JoAnne left her work for an hour and went through a long series of eye exercises which would, the doctor assured her, do much to develop and strengthen the muscles that were weak and "lazy." She worked faithfully, spurred on by the hope that she might see better some day and be rid of the shadows behind which lurked all the nameless fears that haunted her. Ever since her marriage those fears had kept at a distance as if they could not stand the light and happiness of her life. But she had an uneasy consciousness that if Dave weren't there the fears would be. If Dr. Bergner and his dark room and crazy exercises could help any she would do her share by working at them for the year that was prescribed.

Chapter 12

IT WAS A HAPPY YEAR, full of work and plans and fellowship with other young people. At the church they had found other couples working and living under the same circumstances, both employed and one or both of them in night school. All were planning for the day when the apprenticeships would be over and they could buy their own homes. It was the first time JoAnne had been one of a group where young men and woman fellowshiped in work and play, and she found it good. On the first Sunday after they returned from Texas, when the minister gave the invitation for church membership Dave looked down at JoAnne, whispered, "I'm going," and stepped into the aisle. Her eyes filled with tears and her heart sang for joy. They were one now in service for the Master.

When spring came, with the odors of damp earth and the fragrance of spring flowers penetrating even the air of the city, they would spend the Sunday afternoons in the country, seeking out the little used roads and the quiet lanes. These drives brought memories of last year when Nona had been with them.

"If she could have lived out here perhaps she would have been strong. She was always well when we lived at the Home. The air here is so different from the city. Winters would be clean instead of dirty and smoky. And no matter how hot it got it would be fresher than those humid downtown streets."

"Maybe when she gets well we can find her a place out here. Or better still, — oh, listen to this, keeda! Let's buy a place in the country ourselves, — a place with a big sunny room where Nona can rest and grow strong!"

JoAnne gasped. "And turn farmer? Do you know how to farm?"

"Not a bit of it. But I don't have to be a farmer to live in the country. All these places are close enough to a station that a guy could commute. Lots of the men at the store do it. I could go to the store and you could stay at home and make like a farmer!"

"Let's have a garden and some fruit and I'll can dozens of jars of all sorts of things. I know how. I was boss of the canning room the last summer I was at the Home."

"And we'll have some chickens and while I'm in the city laboring to make a living you can peddle eggs up and down the street. I think you'd make a good peddler. I'd probably get arrested for breaking the child labor laws."

"Could I have a kitten, Dave?"

"For a little while."

"Couldn't I keep it? Why?"

"Because kittens turn into cats. JoAnne, if you'll get

those eyes of yours into condition, you can drive me to and from the station. Get busy, keeda!"

So JoAnne worked patiently in the dark room or sat in the chair while the doctor looked through queer glasses and frames at her eyes, and asked questions about the colors and letters on the wall charts. At last, when she had begun to wonder if she would have to spend the rest of her life on this tiresome treadmill, the new glasses came, and Dr. Bergner smiled at her joy.

"They're magic!" she cried, running to the window. "Why, I can see buildings a mile away, I believe. Oh Dave, I want to go out to the lake. I always wanted to see more of it. It ended so soon!"

Then she turned quickly to the doctor. "Can I drive a car, now?"

"Yes, indeed. Never without your glasses, of course. But lots of people are limited that way. Sure! You can drive as well as your husband."

She hurried so quickly down the stairs that even Dave's agile feet could hardly keep up with her. She raced ahead of him to the parking lot and when he unlocked the car door she slipped under his arm and into the driver's seat. Holding out her hand she cried,

"Give me the key, Dave. He said I could drive as well as you."

Dave laughed as he pushed her over and slid under the wheel. "You're a twerp! But I'll give you a driving lesson the next time we go to the country."

To his amazement and delight she learned quickly and seemed to have no sense of fear when driving. When a near accident on a crowded highway called for some quick thinking and intuitive action, she brought them through safely. Her hands on the wheel were steadier than Dave's as he reached for it in the side road into which she had turned.

"You'll do!" he said breathlessly. "Aren't you scared?"

"No. Should I be?"

"I thought you might be. I am. So *you* had better drive home. Hidden away in that little body of yours are the makin's of a real giant."

During that summer he taught her to swim. Here, too, she was fearless. Her glasses had to be left behind, so Dave always swam at her side to give her assurance. At any minute she could touch him, and knew that he could lead her back to shore though she could not see it. She developed speed and endurance and grew strong and tanned in the sun. Watching her progress Dave was glad, believing that all the morbid fears were a thing of the past. Perhaps they had never been as bad as Nona had led him to believe.

Chapter 13

ONLY ONE THING marred the brightness of these months. That was the separation from Nona. She was all that JoAnne had known of love and tenderness during most of her life, and the separation had been a shock. She hoped that before many months Nona could come back and find a small apartment near them, or better yet, that they could buy that home in the country where Nona could have the clean air and sunshine she needed. Each letter from Arizona contained assurances and the promise, "I'll be O.K. before long."

But as the winter came on the letters became shorter and less frequent. JoAnne thought that this meant that Nona had found friends and was too busy with them to write as often as she had done last year. But Dave, after a talk with Miss Moxon, spoke soberly to her of the implications of this change. JoAnne stared at him with startled eyes.

"You mean she won't get well?" she cried with a shrill note of panic in her voice. "Dave, is that what you mean?"

Dave put his arms around her as he answered. "We

can't say that, dear. Of course she *might* get well. As long as she lives there's a chance God will cure her. He could, we know. But we have to be prepared for what may happen. Her nurse wrote to Miss Moxon that she isn't as well as she was in the summer."

'Well, what can they expect? She was always worse in winter, then better when it got hot. I'm not going to believe she is going to — die."

That last word was whispered as she turned to hide her face against Dave's shoulder. He smoothed her hair, and spoke, his voice gruff with feeling.

"Don't you worry. We're both going to believe the best. And next summer when we have our vacations we're going down to see her."

To Miss Moxon he defended himself. "I just couldn't tell her what you said. After all God *could* heal her, couldn't He?"

"I guess He could. But we have no reason to think He will. I haven't heard of Him performing such miracles lately. Well,— when the blow comes it's you that has to manage the youngster. I'm glad she's yours and not mine!"

"So am I, lady! And I think we'll keep on believing."

"Believing is all right. But what you're doing is hiding your face from the dark and trying to tell yourself the sun's shining."

The next letter that came from Nona was longer and had several droll sketches of herself and her companions. JoAnne was cheered, and as the weeks went by she forgot Dave's warning and her fear. In February Miss Moxon was absent from the store, and no one but Dave and Mr. Brantwell knew that she had flown to Arizona to be with Nona.

It was on a gloomy day when the smoke and fog hung so low that midafternoon seemed like night, that Dave came to JoAnne as she sat typing in the office.

"I don't feel very well, and Mr. Brantwell says we can take the rest of the day off."

She looked startled, then covered her machine and got her wraps. Neither spoke in the crowded bus nor as they climbed the stairs. As the door closed behind them she turned quickly.

"Dave, what is it? Did you get hurt? You're never sick."

He held her close and choked as he spoke. "It's Nona, darling. She's — she's gone!"

She stared at him as if without comprehension. Then a shudder passed over her and she would have fallen had it not been for his arms about her. He led her to the davenport and sat talking quietly until she lost some of her rigidity. She did not cry as he had expected. He wished she would. A fellow could do something with tears — wipe them off or kiss them away. But she just lay there, unresponsive to his clumsy efforts to comfort her. He prepared some soup, hoping that the heat would stimulate her. But after the first spoonful she turned wearily away. All evening he sat by her side, stroking her hand as it lay in his or smoothing her hair back from her forehead. At last he spoke.

"Honey, it's almost ten o'clock. I promised Dad I'd call him and tell him what you want him to do."

"To do? What do you mean?"

"About Nona. Do you want them to bring her back here or let her stay there? Dad will do whatever you say."

"I don't want to say. You do it, Dave."

"Do you want to see her?"

She thought for a minute, then spoke through quivering lips. "I don't think I could stand it."

"Then you shan't have to. Let's remember her as she was that last night. We'll tell Dad to have them lay her down there where it's always sunshine. Now I want you to take these two tablets the doctor gave me and go to bed. I'll sit by you until you go to sleep."

For a week they did not return to work. Dave stayed close by, showing his sympathy and concern by his constant and ofttimes clumsy attentions. She seemed to appreciate his nearness, but nothing aroused her from her dull apathy. Even when Miss Moxon returned to the city and came to tell them of those last days and to give them a few trinkets Nona had sent back, she remained listless.

But it was she who suggested that they return to work on Monday, and as she greeted the girls at the office Dave was amazed at her composure. He left her, feeling that they had passed a real crisis and scored a great victory,— that the fears and hysterics had at last been conquered and JoAnne had grown up!

Chapter 14

I<small>T WAS A NIGHT</small> in early March, cloudy and warm. Dave had been struggling for two hours with a paper that had to be turned in the next day, and JoAnne was ironing. The apartment was oppressively hot, and after several unsuccessful attempts to type a correct final paper, Dave flung aside his papers.

"Let's open the windows and then go for a walk. We'd never be able to sleep in this oven! Why couldn't we get this kind of heat out of the furnace in January when we needed it?"

As they came out onto the walk the air seemed heavy with a threat of storm. Dave took JoAnne's hand in his and held it close in the pocket of his coat. They loved to walk this way, and even in the snowy days of winter they would often walk a mile or more after an evening's work. They swung along toward the park whose paths had become familiar to them. Tonight it was deserted. The snow which had attracted boys and girls with their sleds was now gone, and the hill was bare and muddy. The lagoon which, a few weeks before had glittered with whiteness in the moonlight, was a vast area of blackness.

The trees were gaunt skeletons, tossing their branches in the wind like giant arms. Overhead the clouds scudded across the sky, deepening the shadows. Occasionally the moon showed for a few minutes, pale and dull, with an eerie light.

To Dave, as they turned into the path that skirted the lagoon, it was indescribably beautiful. The fresh air was invigorating and he drew it hungrily into his lungs. The darkness was soothing to his tired eyes, and the wind carried a promise of spring that spoke to his country-bred senses. He had not noticed JoAnne's quietness nor the quickening of her steps, until at last she seemed to be almost pulling him.

"Hey! Slow down! Let's stop and rest awhile. Here on this bench."

Obediently she sat down where the shadow of a large evergreen tree lay deep. The water before them looked black and bottomless. Dave talked, glad to be away from his books and out in the night with the girl he loved. At length he noticed her quietness and spoke contritely,

"Keeda, you're not saying a word. I'll keep still. It's your turn now. What's on your mind? Why JoAnne! You're shaking all over. Are you cold, honey?"

She drew in a breath and tried to laugh. But the laugh had a hysterical note that caught Dave's ear and made him uneasy.

"I'm cold all over. I feel like I'd never be warm. I don't like that water. It's so *black*, and the shadows are moving so queerly, and the wind makes me feel hollow, and —"

Her voice was rising and the hysteria was becoming a

reality. Dave rose quickly and turned her away from the lagoon to face the street.

"Come on. Let's go home and fix a snack. I'm hungry as a bear."

He had an impulse to run, for they had often raced together along these paths or on the beach. But he knew that, if she ran, her fear might become that of one pursued. So, talking of commonplaces he led her out to the light of the boulevard, then back to the brightness of their home.

Long after JoAnne was asleep Dave lay thinking of her mood, and a feeling of heartsick realization came over him. Now he knew what Nona had tried to tell him. He knew too, that his confidence that the battle had been won was the confidence of ignorance. He had never seen a case of hysterics, but he knew that JoAnne had been near to the breaking point there by the lagoon. What had caused it? What made her such a bundle of nerves? Had the training at the Home been to blame? Had Nona pampered her into such a state of weakness? He didn't know the answers, but the task of helping her was now his and he'd devote his life to curing her.

He had been sleeping for several hours and when his ears first caught the unusual sound it was hard for him to waken thoroughly. But the sound continued and at last he was startled into awareness. He reached for JoAnne, but at the touch of his hand the sound which had been a moan, became a shrill cry of panic. He snapped on the bed-lamp asking anxiously,

"What is it, dear? Are you sick?"

She did not answer. She was sitting up in bed, her white face and staring eyes telling of some horror that was beyond words. Her whole body was shaking, and Dave reached for a blanket to wrap about her. Again at the touch, a cry seemed wrung from her, and her un-seeing gaze told him that she did not realize who he was. Frantically he shook her, holding his hand over her mouth as another scream seemed imminent. She struggled in his arms for a moment then, as he kept calling her name, ap-peared to waken to a realization of his presence. She clung to him, breaking into deep sobs that tore her body with their intensity. He tried again and again to question her, to discover what had frightened her. She only clung to him and continued to sob. At last, wrapping her in the blanket, he carried her into the living room. He turned on every lamp, that no shadow might oppress her, and sat in the big chair with his arms about her.

It was a half hour before she became quiet enough to talk. By that time Dave knew that neither of them would sleep again. Perhaps it would be better to let her talk. If they could get at the root of the thing, they might be able to effect a cure. He was ready to admit now that Nona had not exaggerated the condition. What a respon-sibility for a young girl to have carried so many years, the care of this neurotic child.

"What's it all about, keeda?" he asked.

"Oh, I can't tell about it. It's so *awful!*"

"What was it? A dream?"

"No, I was awake. But I got to thinking after I woke up."

"Thinking about what, honey? Let's talk it over so I can help you. What thoughts could have made you so frightened?"

She hesitated but he pressed his questions until she began to talk. Bit by bit he drew out the story of her fear — not a fear of any tangible thing, but a great nameless horror that hung over her at times. The uncertainties of the future, possibility of separation from all whom she loved, the chance of physical disaster,— these were not feared in themselves. But back of them all hung that terrible unknown fear. It lurked in the black depths of the lagoon, it moaned in the wind on cloudy nights, and it spoke to her of Nona's lonely grave in Arizona.

"When did this thing start?" Dave asked gravely.

"I don't know *when* I first felt it. It seems I've always had it. It must have come from something that happened before I was old enough to remember. Nona said I was terrible when I first went to the Home. If I could just remember what it is, I think I wouldn't be afraid any more. Sometimes I am just on the verge of remembering, then it's gone again. At the moment when I think I have hold of it, it's not there and everything gets black and I almost faint."

"Don't try to remember it then! Concentrate on trying to forget it. You've been doing fine. I thought you were all over it."

"Nona told you about it, didn't she?"

"Yes. She knew she had to. But don't you get discouraged, keeda. We'll lick it yet. For a year and a half you've been free from it, and that shows it can be done."

"But it always comes back, Dave. And I know it's always in the shadows and storm, just waiting. If I could only remember!"

For an hour longer he talked to her quietly, promising

that she need not fear for he would be with her always to stand between her and anything that might frighten her. The future could not be fearsome for they would be in it together. Listening, she grew calm. As the first light began to show in the sky he spoke quickly,

"Let's get dressed in a jiffy, JoAnne. There's going to be a sunrise soon. Let's beat it to the lake shore!"

Soon they were racing through the dawn, and ahead of them down the long vista of the boulevard, a roseate sunrise colored the sky. Later, as he left her at her office and turned toward his own, Dave drew a weary sigh.

"No wonder Nona used to come to work looking done in at times. But the poor leeta, beeta keeda! She has to be taken care of. Dave, old boy, you've picked you out quite a job. You have to take care that nothing *ever* happens to bring on another spell like that."

Chapter 15

HAPPINESS is a wonderful tonic and beautifier. Dave was true to his resolution. In every possible way he guarded JoAnne's habits and even her thoughts. He never left her alone. On the evenings that he attended school she was with him. The courses she took in interior decorating and English were a joy and inspiration to her. As the weeks became months, and the months in their circuits rolled into years, she lost the hesitant manner and lack of poise that had betrayed her immaturity, and developed a charm and graciousness that amazed even Dave. With them came a beauty that he had not anticipated. The JoAnne of the misty street corner was a rather plain child. The JoAnne of their fifth anniversary was a beautiful woman.

Dave came back into the kitchen with his overcoat on, to drain his last cup of coffee and to kiss JoAnne good-by.

"I'm going to miss you at the store today, little lady. But I'm mighty happy to have reached this milestone. I've got a wife now instead of a career gal. What are you going to do all day? I hope you don't have to go out in this weather."

"Not even to the store. I'm going to celebrate my freedom by cleaning the hall closet."

"Well, don't break your neck reaching for that top shelf. And don't throw out any of my things. I'll do my own weeding. And don't forget to be all prettied up when I get home. We're going out tonight to celebrate five years of happiness. Life's great, isn't it?"

He grabbed her for a hug and kiss, then dashed for the door. As he reached it he turned to call back a final admonition,

"If you do go out, don't forget your extra glasses!"

Then he was off, clearing the stairs three steps at a time and landing on the sidewalk all set for the sprint for the bus at the corner. As he swung on he turned for a last wave at JoAnne in the window.

Pretty good kind of a life, he thought as he crowded into a space by the back door. It seemed a bit queer to be going without JoAnne after having her with him for five years. But he was mighty glad she did not have to work any more. He was through school now. The debts from his mother's illness and death were all paid, and the last raise he'd had was a good one. He could take care of JoAnne now like a guy *should* take care of his wife. They could maybe make a down payment on a place in the suburbs in the spring. There'd be a garden and some fruit trees, some chickens and a cat. And there'd be a big shady yard where a playpen could be put in sight of the kitchen windows. He would build a sand box and put up a swing. Pretty swell life, this was!

He looked at his watch as he swung off the bus, and

decided that he could spare a few minutes to look at the progress the workmen were making on the excavation for the new addition to the store. They were all hoping to surprise Dad by having the excavating finished by the time he came back from that buying trip to Europe. The huge machinery was a continual object of interest to passersby, as the giant shovel dug into the earth. If he hurried he would have five minutes to spare for this fascinating sport. If he ever had a son he hoped they'd watch things like this together. He turned the corner and joined the crowd that had gathered by the barricade around the vast excavation.

* * * * * *

JoAnne was singing happily about her work. The realization that she was free to spend the hours of each day working in her own home, with no demands on her except those of a housewife, gave her a feeling of elation. As long as she could remember, even back in the days when she had stood on a box to wash silverware while Nona dried it, she had dreamed of a home where she could cook and sew and clean, where she could arrange and rearrange the furniture and where she could do just as she pleased with her own possessions. That dream had had a partial fulfillment when she and Nona had rented and furnished this apartment. Those had been happy days. But there had never been enough time to care for things as they desired. Cooking and cleaning were wearisome after a trying day in the office. Even these last five years, the happiest she had ever known, had been too full for leisurely homemaking.

But now she was free! Last night she had left Brant-well's forever. Hereafter she would be just Mrs. David Robertson, housewife, homemaker, and — someday, per-haps — mother of sons and daughters who would grow up in a real home.

As she dusted the pictures on the bookcase she looked lovingly at one of Nona. Vivid memory of their years together came to her, but the pain that used to come with such memories had softened with the years, and was no longer pain but sweetness and deep appreciation of all Nona had done for her.

"You were a wonderful big sister," she whispered. "Where you are now I hope you know how happy I am, for I owe it all to you. And I hope you know that Dave picked up where you left off. Between you, you managed to fix up my eyes and stiffen my backbone and make a woman of me,— I *hope*." The last two words were more a thought than speech, for she was determined not to put into speech the doubt. She had come victoriously through more than three years. Surely there would be no relapse!

Next to Nona's picture stood one of herself and Dave, taken during that wonderful week on Dad Brantwell's ranch five years ago. They had it taken to send to Nona so that she might share some of the good time they were having. They had sent books, fruit and flowers, but she had liked the picture best and when Amy Moxon had re-turned after Nona had gone, she had brought this with her. Looking at it now JoAnne thought,

"What a pair of children we were! Even Dave has changed a lot since then. Why I look like an under-sized eighth grader! No wonder they all thought Dave was my big brother. I hope I've changed *altogether* in these five years."

Before the mirror she studied herself. No,— no one would think her an eighth grader now. She wished she were larger, but that couldn't be helped. And in spite of her size she was definitely no longer a child. Nona's "little sister" had become Dave's "favorite wife."

A ring at the bell startled her, and when she answered, Miss Moxon's voice called, "May I come up?"

JoAnne pressed the buzzer and waited at the head of the stairs. What was Amy Moxon doing here at this hour? Surely she knew that JoAnne wasn't ill, but had quit the store for good. The nurse stepped inside the door and for a minute did not speak. Then, putting her arm around JoAnne's shoulder she said,

"You'll have to come with me, dear. Dave has been hurt and the doctor wants you with him. No," she said quickly, "he isn't too bad. At least, we don't think so. But he may want you. So get your things," she added as JoAnne stood stonily, "and I'll go with you. My car is outside."

As they rode JoAnne roused enough to ask a few questions and Miss Moxon answered simply and directly. She didn't know exactly what had happened. She had just opened her office when one of the boys came for her. As clearly as she could piece together the story there had been an accident with one of the giant excavators, and it had toppled as it was being taken from the pit. Dave must have seen the danger before anyone else, for he had cried out and leaped over the wooden barrier to jerk a workman out of the way. The man was all right but the machine had struck Dave and knocked him into the excavation. The machine had caught his feet under it as it fell, and when Miss Moxon got there they had just released him and were starting for the hospital.

"I really don't know how badly he is hurt. The mud in the pit was very soft and there may be no serious damage at all. But he asked for you and Dr. Herman promised I'd get you. You'll try to be quiet when you see him won't you, JoAnne? Even if it isn't serious it will be a big help if you'll be brave about it."

"Of course I will."

She *was* brave. Her heart seemed to stop beating when she saw him, and for a moment everything was black before her eyes. But he was watching her and she couldn't let him down! So she kept her voice quiet, and her hand was firm as it held his. They were just taking him to the emergency room, so, after a long look into his eyes and a kiss on his lips she let him go.

Chapter 16

After he had been wheeled away she sat alone in the small adjoining room into which the nurse had led her. While the slow minutes ticked away her tortured mind tried to picture what they were doing to him. Amy Moxon had said it wasn't bad, but she might not know. It *could* be bad even though Dave had smiled at her when she came. He had looked pale and there was a funny sound to his voice when he said her name. What if Dave were hurt so badly that he wouldn't get well?

For an hour that seemed like ten, she paced the room, staring first from one window at the traffic in an alley and from the other where she could catch a glimpse of the lake. If Dave didn't get well, what would she do? There wouldn't be anyone left to her. How *could* she stand it? She could remember dimly the day when a man in a car had taken her mother away. She had cried a long time, and then — she could not remember how — Nona had been there to comfort her, and through all the years at the Home had never failed her. When Nona had had to leave Dave had come. She had never learned to live without one of them at hand. Could she do it now?

Out across the lake a dark cloud was rolling up. The wind had risen and the lake looked dull and angry. She thought she could hear the waves pound on the beach. She tried to busy herself with a magazine or to watch the alley where trucks were delivering merchandise to the back doors of shops. But she kept returning to the window. She knew she should not, but it drew her back. Gazing on it she felt terror creeping over her. All the fears that had been held in check for years gathered to assail her now. She turned from the window and sat down in a chair. She dared not scream though the desire was strong in her. She did not hear the sounds in the hall nor see the nurses pass to and fro. That terrible oppression of fear, that unknown something that was too strong for her to fight hovered over her. She sat tense with panic, her cold hands twisted together and her eyes staring. As she was losing consciousness she heard a voice.

"Child! Why, you're just ready to faint. Here, Martha, help me." Then strong arms lifted her, she was laid on a bed and complete oblivion came.

She wakened to find a kindly Negro face bending over and a tender voice talking in soothing tones.

"Thas better, honey. Jus' you take this, now. It's some warm milk, good for you. You went clean out for a lil' minute an' you need this. I guess you b'longs to that boy jus' come out —"

"Oh, are they through with him? May I see him?"

"After while I guess. We'll jus' have to wait. I'm not a nurse. I'm jus' an aid. So I don' know. Maybe I can find out. You jus' rest here and I'll see 'bout it."

Somehow just those soothing tones seemed to wrap her

about and promise comfort and security. So JoAnne lay quietly waiting, and hoping that the Negro woman would come back. When she did it was to say hurriedly,

"They want you, honey, cause he's comin' out the ether. He's callin' you. The nurse says you mus' be quiet. Jus' come so's he can see you. An' you're not to cry. You can do thet?"

"Yes, I can. If I can just see him I'll be quiet as a mouse. I promise."

The knowledge that she could see Dave, that there was something she could do for him, was a stimulant. The fear of imaginary things was gone. Dave's need was a real thing, and her whole being yearned to fill that need. She followed the aid with a steady step and gave Miss Moxon and Dr. Herman a reassuring smile when they met her at the door of Dave's room. She wanted them to know that they need not worry about her!

Even when she saw that Dave did not know her she did not falter, but sat down by the bed. He was moaning and the sound cut through her. Timidly at first, then more courageously as the nurse did not object, she took his hand and held it in both her own. At once the moaning stopped although the restless eyes still sought something.

"Speak to him," said the nurse softly.

At the sound of her voice he turned toward her, and although he did not seem to recognize her he lay still, drifting off at least into sleep. All day she sat there. The nurses came and went, occasionally giving Dave an injection and watching carefully every movement he made. An orderly brought in an easier chair and they propped

JoAnne in it with pillows all around her. A nurse brought a tray for her at supper time, and with one hand she managed to eat a small portion of food and drink a cup of strong coffee. The other hand still held Dave's. If she tried to take it away the moaning began again.

As the hours wore on her back ached and she became faint with weariness, but she dared not move. Then when she felt that she could bear it no longer, an arm came around her. A rich soft voice spoke soothingly,

"Jus' you let loose an' res' awhile, honey. You're fagged. Jus' let loose an' relax. I'll hol' you an' you can hol' that boy's han'."

JoAnne did relax, and as she settled comfortably against the broad shoulder her very weary brain registered the thought, 'Why, it's that dear Negro mammy again!'

She slept a bit but wakened at Dave's first movement. Hour after hour passed. Several doctors came in, watching awhile and then going out after a consultation with the nurse. Then Dr. Herman came back, and sat by the other side of the bed, his hand often on Dave's wrist, his face intent and inscrutable.

As the first gray streaks of dawn began to lighten the sky, Dave stirred and opened his eyes. They were still dull and without comprehension until he saw JoAnne. Then a half smile twisted his lips and his weak voice spoke.

"Hello, keeda."

"Hello, dear."

"What are you doing? Why don't you come on to bed?"

"I'm not ready yet, Dave."

He lay quietly for a time, then spoke again, more weakly. "I can't see you. Come closer, JoAnne. Where are you?"

She leaned over him and spoke reassuringly, "I'm here, dear. Now go to sleep again. I won't go away."

The doctor felt the pulse again, then hurriedly gave another injection. JoAnne, watching the slow rise and fall of the blankets thought several times that the breathing had stopped. She seemed to be two people. One of her was quiet and strong and was holding Dave's hand, sending her strength into his heart and body. The other one was wondering how long she could go on without screaming and what she would do when that breathing stopped.

The heavy eyelids lifted again, and the faint voice spoke so softly that she had to lean closely to catch the words.

"Is — it — morning? — Where's — the — sunrise?"

JoAnne looked toward the window. Only the gray western sky was visible above the dark outlines of ugly buildings. She wished they were in an east room where the sunrise might be seen when it came.

"Come — on,— keeda. Let's — go — and — see —"

The voice died away and the doctor reached again for the limp hand. JoAnne saw his eyes meet those of the nurse, and knew what the look meant. They were wrong! Dave *wasn't* going to die! She slid from the chair and fell on her knees beside the bed, holding that right hand against her breast. With her eyes fixed on Dave's troubled ones she began to talk.

She talked of the sunrise, of the mornings when they had raced along the sand and had stood with bare heads catching the morning breeze and gazing at the brilliance of dawn over the lake. She told of sunrise on the ranch, where they had ridden horseback to see it from a rise in the plain. She described a sunrise they had seen through the trees in the park, with the birds singing a morning roundelay as accompaniment. Then she began to promise more sunrises. She reminded him of their plan for a home in the country.

"We'll have a sunrise of our own then, Dave. When we pick out a home it will face the east and we'll have a vista of trees making a lane that leads right into the sunrise."

On and on she talked. If Dave wanted a sunrise she would make one for him! She would make one out of their memories and their dreams. And all the time the doctor held his fingers on Dave's left wrist, while his face and the face of the nurse grew more sober.

Behind her JoAnne could hear the Negro woman praying in a way that showed her nearness to the God she besought. JoAnne did not pray. She did not have time. She had to make a sunrise for Dave to keep him from slipping away. Yet all the time she talked she felt the uselessness of it. Dave was going and she could not hold him. She could not even give him a real sunrise.

Then, when her heart was heavy with foreboding and her voice weak with strain, the colored woman spoke in an awed tone.

"Looka, honey. It *is* a sunrise! There in the west window!"

106

JoAnne looked. It was true. The sunrise colors had spread to encircle the entire horizon. Through the west window it could be seen,— not so flamboyant as in the east, but with a softer, purer coloring that was indescribably beautiful. She turned to the bed, and still holding Dave's hand spoke insistently.

"Dave! — — Dave! Wake up, dear, and see the sunrise!"

He did not stir and the doctor bent closer. Again and again she spoke. The Negro was praying and the student nurse had turned away. Miss Moxon had bowed her head and was biting her lip.

"Come on, Dave! Wake up, darling. It's sunrise!"

A long shuddering breath came, then the dear eyes opened. Gently JoAnne turned his eyes to face the window, and as the rosy streaks colored the roofs and chimneys, a glad smile lighted his face.

"It is sunrise, isn't it, keeda? A wonderful — sunrise."

The last word was a whisper and his eyes closed again. But the breathing went on, growing stronger and easier minute by minute. The doctor watched awhile, gave a stimulant, and after another hour said with a satisfied smile,

"That's better. The pulse is steady now, and this little lady needs a rest. Martha, will you fix her up close by? We may need her again. For the present, nurse and I will carry on."

Chapter 17

In a few days Dave had rallied from shock sufficiently to go through the long series of examinations to determine the extent of his injuries. JoAnne was spending every day with him, but at night she went back to the apartment, accompanied by Miss Moxon.

"I promised Dave I'd do this," that friend said. "I am sure that you could stay alone, but I'm also sure Dave would worry. So I'm letting a friend use my room for a few weeks and I'm going to live with you in your snug nest. It's a lovely apartment, JoAnne. You have the gift of homemaking. I can see it everywhere."

"I love this place," answered JoAnne. "Nona and I had it first. We started with nothing and fixed it up as we could afford. Dave and I have bought new things as we needed them. We've tried to get good pieces so that we can take them with us when we get our own home."

"I'm glad you're planning that. Get an extra room for me so that I can get out of this filthy city."

"Oh, we'll do that! We used to plan a room for Nona, but that dream didn't come true. So we'll fix one for you."

To JoAnne those days were a time of rejoicing that the first danger was past, and a time of apprehension concerning the future. There were days of relief, as when the doctor said that in spite of a temporary paralysis there was no permanent injury to the spine. And there were times of heartache when she learned that both feet had been crushed and that it would be a long time before Dave walked again.

"How can I stand to see him quiet for so long?" she thought miserably, as she rode home on the bus one night. "It hurts terribly to think of Dave's feet being still."

In spite of the hours of depression, however, she did not feel again the terror she had felt that first day. Each day when she reached the hospital he was waiting for her with a smile on his face and a cheery "Hello" on his lips. With Dave's spirit upholding her even from a hospital bed, she was not afraid. She carefully concealed from him any discouragement, and let him see only that she was confident of a future, not too distant, when they would be back in the apartment, planning a home in the country.

They longed for the presence and comfort of Mr. Brantwell, for he had become to them as a dear relative who took the place of the parents they did not have. But he was seriously ill in a New York hospital. Mr. Slade, the vice-president of the firm, had hurried east as soon as the news was received, but had been denied entrance to the sickroom. Even news of the store was forbidden, and rumor was rife that the eccentric old man would never be back among his employees.

Day after day JoAnne made her journeys to the hospital, each day assuring herself staunchly that Dave was "much better today." There were also bewildering conferences with Mr. Slade, the insurance adjuster, and the contractor whose machine caused the damage. She always left these conferences in a state of utter confusion and distrust. She had no confidence in her own understanding of the situation. She did not know the meaning of the terms they used. And as the days passed she began to distrust the men she was dealing with. At last she spoke to Amy Moxon about her feeling that even Mr. Slade did not have Dave's interest at heart.

"Humpf!" snorted that capable friend. "I didn't like it when Slade undertook to represent Dave in that affair. If Dad had been here it would have been different. Dad knows that Slade is not fond of Dave."

"Not fond of Dave! Why?"

Miss Moxon laughed. "Is it so amazing that there is someone on earth who isn't in love with Dave?"

"No, of course not," JoAnne said in embarrassment. "But why should he dislike him enough to not help now?"

"Could be he's jealous."

"Jealous? Why should a vice-president be jealous of a young personnel man?"

"Probably because he realizes, as many of us do, that Dad's eye — and heart — are fixed on Dave."

"I still don't think he should —"

"Neither do I. Tomorrow I am going to talk to Dr. Herman. Maybe he can suggest something. Maybe he can get Dad's lawyer on the job."

None of these problems were taken to the hospital. No matter how heavy her heart, she always greeted Dave with a smile, and when he asked questions she had sufficiently satisfying answers to allay any doubts he might have. As yet, none of their friends from the store or the church were allowed to see him, so she had all the visiting hours to herself. Sometimes she read to him, often she talked, but usually she just sat holding his hand while he slept or lay in a half-sleeping, half-waking daze. Each evening she told him good-by she would go home to fall into bed so wearily that she had no problem of wakefulness. Morning always brought with it the promise of being with him in a few hours. She marked off each day on the kitchen calendar, and felt like celebrating when she tore off a page.

The nurses and aids at the hospital grew accustomed to her prompt arrival each day, and recognized the lift that her presence gave to the patient. Of them all the colored aid Martha was on hand most frequently to help in any way she could. She seemed to know without being told just what could bring relief. JoAnne wondered if she ever took time off, for she appeared to be on duty day and night.

"I'm puttin' in all the time I can jus' now. Jawn — he's my man — an' me, we savin' all we can. Someday we buy a home out where they's grass for the kids. I can't always work daytimes, cause they's seven of them kids an' they bear watchin'. But my mammy's visitin' me now an' she takes care of 'em. While she's here I make it count." Then she would hurry away humming under her breath.

There came a time when the doctors grew grave again, when Dave was restless and pain-burdened once more. And the week before Christmas she stood bravely smiling as they wheeled him away for another trip to surgery, this time knowing that the poor useless feet would have to be removed in order that Dave's life might be spared. She had almost fainted when they told her, but she had rallied and walked into his room to greet him with a smile, and to sit with him until they took him away. She watched them down the hall, and did not move until the elevator door had shut. Then she turned blindly, to find Martha at her side.

"Honey, I'm jus' goin' off duty for an hour. Want to go to the chapel with me? They'll be quite some time upstairs. I get you back here in plenty of time."

"I — I — don't know."

"Better come on. It's a good place to rest."

Obediently she went. The chapel was small and quiet, and Martha's voice as she prayed brought a sense of calm. JoAnne wished she could pray. With Dave up there so terribly in need she *ought* to pray. But she couldn't. She felt so dull and tired that she could not make such effort. It was nice for Martha to pray, and it did seem to help. But for herself, she could not feel that God was near at all. As she listened to Martha's voice it reminded her of the times she and Nona had prayed together. Nona was always so much in earnest that God seemed very near. She and Dave had kept up their church-going, and they always had a short devotional together before retiring. But she had never poured out her heart like Nona did. And now with Nona gone and Dave up there in the

113

operating room, God was not near at all. She felt cold and sick and terribly alone.

Martha went on, "An' Lord, dear Lord, show these dear chil'run Thy great and unchangeable and matchless love even in this day of sorrow. Show them that the sorrow can be turned into joy, and that even the pain that comes from Thy han' can be a cause of rejoicin'. Comfort them and give them stren'th. We ask this in the name of Thy own dear Son who bore such agonizin' pain for us. Amen."

Martha rose from her knees and put one arm about JoAnne's shoulders.

"Let's go up now, honey. I promised the doctor I'd wait with you, and don't forget the Lord will be waitin' with us."

Again that night JoAnne was allowed to stay at Dave's side, and they fought and won a second battle against death. In the middle of the next day, when the mists had cleared from his mind, he reached for her hand and grinned.

"Hello, keeda! This time next year they tell me I'll be hopping escalators on two pegs!"

She drew a long breath and her heart leaped with joy. Dave was still on top of the world! She smiled back with the answer she knew he expected.

"All we have to do now is get you well again. And we're on our way, aren't we?"

Chapter 18

THEY WERE DEFINITELY on their way, for Dave grew stronger every day. But it was not a clear road even yet. They did not know how long it might be nor where it might lead. The paralysis, which the doctors repeatedly assured her was only temporary, lingered and JoAnne's heart was wrung afresh every day at the sight of the inert figure under the blanket. Such passiveness was utterly alien to the memory of the agile Dave who had run up and down the escalators and hopped the shippers' trucks for a stolen ride. But his spirits were buoyant and when she was in his presence she was happy and hopeful.

A few of his friends were permitted to see him, and he greeted them gaily, overcoming their sympathetic embarrassment with his cheery optimism.

"I'm just taking a well-earned rest. I'll be back among you before you know it."

JoAnne was growing weary in body from the long trips to and from the hospital, and from the strain of keeping her discouragement from showing. If Dave could be gay and happy in such circumstances, she wasn't going to let him down, no matter how glum she felt. So Dave talked of their plans and of the dream home in the country. And she smiled and planned with him and drew courage from him.

Dr. Herman stopped her one day as she was leaving, and drew her aside into the end of the hall where two easy chairs gave an opportunity for relaxation. After questioning her about herself for a few minutes, during which time he noted that the weeks of tension had not wearied her as much as he feared, he broached the subject of Dave's return home.

"All we can do now is to wait. Dave is in perfect health except for that paralysis, and time alone will remedy that. If you could care for him at home, he could go tomorrow. Just being back with you will be a tonic and may give him the boost that will do the business. But here's the snag. I want his present treatments to continue, for the massaging is necessary if we want those nerves to function again and the muscles to remain healthy. We must not let them atrophy while we wait."

"Couldn't I care for him?"

"Decidedly not. You've been a good soldier thus far, but this is beyond your strength. It calls for a long period of real labor twice a day, and you're not up to it. I wish I knew of a strong practical nurse."

"Wouldn't that cost a lot of money?"

"Quite a lot. But it's vital. By the way, how do you stand on money, little lady? Is the store paying Dave's salary?"

"Yes. They can't do it indefinitely, however. Mr. Slade warned me about that last week."

"Slade, eh? Humpf! I wish Brantwell were here."

"So do I. But he isn't, and Mr. Slade says he probably will never be able to go to the store again."

"Have you any other source of funds?"

"Well, the contractor has paid all the hospital bills, but he won't pay any more than that until his insurance company says so. We don't know when that will be. Mr. Slade thinks we'd better not depend on it. Dave had accident insurance which will help a lot but it won't last long if Dave can't get back to work. We have a few hundred in savings."

'Good! Don't worry. Dave is really in fine condition and we are all confident a few more weeks will get those legs to working again. Then he will adapt himself to the new feet in no time at all. You can't keep a chap like him down."

"Oh! I'm so glad. I was afraid—"

"Don't be afraid. I'll get to work looking for that nurse or masseur, and as soon as I find one we'll bring the boy home. By the way, don't talk to him about the money side of this affair. Let him think the insurance is taking care of you. By the time he is well enough to take hold again that will be settled and he need not be worried. And don't you worry."

But JoAnne did worry. She knew what the doctor did not,— that Mr. Slade had said that they could not pay Dave's salary after this month. The few hundred dollars in the bank would melt quickly before the expense of a full-time nurse, and the insurance company seemed in no hurry to make a settlement. All night long she tossed and turned as she pondered the problem. She added, sub-tracted, divided and multiplied until the figures whirled in her brain. She and Dave had always budgeted carefully, and she knew exactly how much it would cost them just to keep the apartment and live as plainly as possible. Dave's insurance and the nest egg would do it until fall. Surely Dave would be well by then! But how could he get well if he did not have the right care, and how could he get that care? Their money just wouldn't stretch that far. She'd be willing to eat almost nothing herself, but Dave wouldn't permit that. She tried to think of some work she could do at home and still care for Dave. But no ideas came. Try as she would she could not make the budget balance.

She started for the hospital next day with a heavy heart. Her head ached and she felt logy from lack of sleep. She discovered that her shoes needed soling, and the bright March sunshine brought out the shabbiness of her winter coat. She felt inadequate for the heavy task of living. How could she go on? And what was the use of trying? She never had been equal to meeting difficulties, and it did not seem right for her to have to face such a tangle as her life had become, without Dave to help her. Why should the doctor not want her to talk their affairs over with Dave? He felt fine now, and he would *want* to discuss their problems with her.

But Dr. Herman had spoken sternly and she dared not go against his orders. The whole prospect so frightened her that she wanted to run away from it all, back to the Home if need be, where everything was decided for her and she had no responsibility greater than dishwashing and bed-making. Wearily she climbed the steps and turned toward the elevator.

Dr. Herman met her as she stepped off. Apparently he had been waiting for her. He motioned her to one side and then led her into his office and closed the door.

"Don't be frightened," he said as he noticed her look of alarm. "Nothing has happened to Dave. He's feeling better every day, and we're all mighty pleased. He's waiting for you now so I must not detain you. I just want to do a little prying into your affairs so that we can decide what is to be done for Dave. From our little chat yesterday I gathered that the money for Dave's care is bothering a bit. Can you tell me without stopping to figure just what we can count on?"

Glad to share her problem with the kindly old doctor, and feeling that if he knew it he would surely know what to do about it, she told him everything,— that Mr. Slade, in charge at the store, said Dave's salary must be stopped at the end of this month, the amount of Dave's insurance, how much was in their savings account, how much rent they paid, and what it cost to feed them.

"I figured it all night long," she said. "There will be just about enough to run us until fall, with less than a hundred left for miscellaneous items and a nurse. You know that wouldn't hire a nurse for a month."

He had been writing the figures as she gave them, and now he scanned them closely, whistling under his breath and appearing not to notice the tears in her eyes.

"Let me keep these," he said at last. "I want to see what I can figure out. I am going to have a little talk with Mr. Slade. Then I have another idea I'll talk to you about later. Run along to Dave, now. Don't mention anything to him until we're all set. We're going to work this all out for Dave's good, and you don't need to worry."

"If we can only pull through until fall, Dave will be able to work, won't he? Or if he isn't I could go back to the store then, I'm sure."

"We'll think about that when the time comes. Now trot along. And on the way pick up a smile for Dave."

She did better than that. She gave the doctor a smile, and said hesitantly as she turned away,

"If I had a father I'd want him to be like you."

For a week nothing more was said, and JoAnne began to wonder if they had been forgotten. With the first of the month Dave's salary check came, with a note saying that it would continue until the contractor's Insurance Company had made an adjustment. That lifted some of the load of her worry. Apparently Dr. Herman had had a talk with Mr. Slade. And he would probably take care of the other matters as well.

Then one day she was called into another conference, this time with the doctor and Martha.

"JoAnne, Martha and I think we have worked out the problem of how to care for Dave. We need your cooperation and consent."

"Why,— I'd do anything for Dave! If you're just sure it will be right for him."

"We've looked at it from all angles and we have decided it would be the best thing that could be done. Would you be willing to give up that apartment you like so well, and go to live in a much less pleasant place for Dave's sake?"

"Yes, oh, yes! I'd go and live in the stockyards if it would help him."

Martha who had been standing silently by, laughed heartily, and the doctor chuckled.

"This will be much better than the stockyards. You see the hospital owns a group of buildings a few blocks away. Some day we're going to have a new building there. Just now it is rented as small apartments. Martha's husband takes care of them for us and they live in one of the buildings. In that same building is a three-room apartment that we can vacate for you. Martha can keep an eye on you and Martha's husband, John, can give Dave the treatments he must have."

"Would it really be all right? Can he do it?"

"Martha says he can, and if she says so I believe it."

"What about the cost?"

"The rent will be about one third of what you are now paying. And as John is close he can drop in to give Dave those massages morning and evening at a price that will not be too much. I think this is just the thing to be done. With Martha to oversee you, and John to help Dave, it's an ideal situation."

As Martha left the office in answer to a call, she paused by JoAnne's chair to say, "I hope it won't shock you none to live close to us. Mr. Dave said the other day that his folks came from the south. Maybe my grammaw took care of his grammaw when they was little."

JoAnne laughed shakily. "Maybe she did. And I'll be happy to have you take care of us. I think God sent you."

"I *know* He did," said Martha calmly. "I asked Him to make a way so's I could help you. This is it."

After she had gone down the hall, Dr. Herman said as he showed JoAnne to the door, "It's too bad Martha hasn't an R.N. She's worth two nurses. Some nurses are trained, and some are just born that way. Martha was a born nurse, then she had a year of training in the south and has been soaking up knowledge and skill ever since. And she teams up with God for all her work. It's quite a combination."

"I hope her husband is as good."

"According to her, he's better. That remains to be proved. But we'll take her word for it. She's never let me down. You make a date with her to go over and see the place. Then tell Dave about it after it's all fixed up. Make it as soon as possible for he's ready to go home."

Chapter 19

IN AN AFTERNOON in early April when the lake was sparkling in the spring sunshine and the forsythia by the hospital steps was laden with gold, Dave was taken home. He drew a long breath of the clean air before the ambulance door closed.

"Same old ozone!" he said with a wry smile. "And I've lost a whole winter somewhere. Five months gone!"

He had accepted the new arrangement with his customary good humor and had signed the sublease to their old apartment with a nonchalant air. JoAnne wondered how he could. Her own hand was shaky and her eyes blurred with tears. She had had so much happiness in those rooms!

Dave was silent as they carried him into the new home and so tired from the trip that the doctor gave him a sedative before he left him.

It was, as Martha said, not much of a place as the world might measure it. JoAnne had felt almost sick when she first saw it. But she had brought most of her furniture and had arranged it as nearly as possible like the other apartment. The only difference in the living room was the hospital bed which was placed by the window. When Dave wakened that second morning it was as if he were lying on the davenport and looking on the old familiar room.

"I suppose the outside is different," he said, as they ate breakfast together with her chair pulled up to the little table by his bedside. "But with that vinegar jug lamp, and those red drapes and my books over there, and with the same cook gal I used to have, it sure feels like home!"

This block of old houses had once been on the level with the street, but when the pavement was put in the street had been graded up four feet, leaving the old houses below it. Sad-looking old places they were. Expecting to tear them down in a few years, the hospital trustees had spent on them only such an amount as was necessary to make them livable. Nothing had been spent on paint or landscaping. The front yards which lay between the houses and the street had never been graded into smoothness since the paving had been done. Piles of clay and gravel were undisturbed by rake or spade. Refuse which blew down was not easily removed, and in time the areas which once had been lawns became ugly holes which no one considered it worthwhile to improve.

The back yards, however, were large with at least one tree in each. And over these yards swarmed children. Each house seemed to contain at least a score.

"It was the trees an' yards that decided us should we come here," confided Martha to JoAnne as they stood on the back porch and watched the children play cop and robber in the alley. "I was raised in all outdoors an' I couldn't nohow stand seein' my children cooped up. An'

124

Jawn did need a kind of job that'd help out when he wasn' givin' lessons. When I heard two of the doctors talkin' one day about they needed somebody to look after things here till they was ready to tear it down, I told them to tell the board we'd do it. An' we been doin' it ever since. Someday we goin' own a home with a big yard of our own. Till then I thank the Lord every night for this."

"I thank Him for it, too. I'd live in a much worse place than this and be happy if it would help Dave get well. That's what this place is going to do."

"You're right it is. Jawn an' I are both goin' to pray for that an' Jawn is goin' rub for all he's worth. An' fore you know it Mr. Dave will be walkin' on them new feet."

"Oh, thank you for believing that. It makes me feel more confident to know that someone else believes it too."

"Well, I do. It may be a few months, but they soon go by, an' while we waitin' we'll be workin'. I don' see no use in this place bein' so untidy even if it is old. It's gotta be different if I live here. This back yard is nice. We'll plant some flowers 'longside the fence next change of the moon an' I'll have the boys whitewash the fence. Ain't nothing like whitewash to clean up a place."

"I wish there were something we could do for the front yard. That's the only view Dave will have most of the time, and it's pretty bad."

"Right it is. But we'll fix that too. I'll make Lute an' Jud level it off an' I'll plant castor beans on both sides to hide the neighbors shif'less mess. Castor beans grow fast. Then we'll make a terrace out of that grade up to the walk. They's lots of quick-growin' flowers an' greeny we can put there. It'll be our private park."

JoAnne's voice was excited. "Can we, really? The board won't care, will they?"

"Course not. They better be glad to have us clean this place 'fore the city gets after 'em."

"And do you think maybe we could sometimes,— somehow — carry Dave out so he could see the trees and backyard too?"

"I wouldn' be s'prised. In fac', I already got an' idea. I'll have Jawn an' the boys make a ramp like in the Union Station, and we'll jus' wheel Mr. Dave right out every sunny day!"

"You're so good to us, Martha! I don't know how we would have managed without you. God must have sent you to take care of us."

"Course He did. I tol' you that. He does all my sendin'. I learned a long time ago to quit runnin' ahead on my own. I take my orders from Him, an' it's sure an easy to live. He told me definite to take care of you."

Just how seriously Martha took such orders was evident in the care that she and her "Jawn" lavished on the young couple that had, as Dave expressed it, "been left on their doorstep." Martha began at once to bring orderliness and beauty out of the rubble and ruin about them. Under her supervision her two oldest boys cleared the trash from the back yard, fixed the fence and reset the clothesline posts. They spaded the ground and Martha planted seeds. The small plot in front was cleared and smoothed and graded up to the walk. John built a railing by the steps and a trellis by Dave's window.

"In no time at all we have morning glories," gloated Martha.

John's great size and strength enabled him to care for Dave with little apparent effort, and his tenderness made the massages a less painful ordeal than JoAnne had thought possible. Morning and evening he worked for an hour on the limbs which gave back no response to the persistent rubbing. As he worked he sang softly in a rich sweet baritone that lulled Dave to sleep on those evenings when sleep had threatened to be illusive. He did not talk as much as Martha did, but when he spoke to the children their response was prompt, and there was no questioning of his authority. His speech, except for a pleasing softening of his R's was that of an educated gentleman. He explained to Dave one day when he had had to correct a bit of faulty grammar from one of the boys.

"I don't like to be always after them, but if they learn to speak correctly now they will do it all their lives. But if I let them get away with it now they will never learn. That's Martha's trouble. She knows what is right, but her parents were uneducated and the habits of speech she learned in childhood aren't easily broken."

"Martha hasn't as much education as you have, has she?" queried Dave.

"Not quite. She has been through high school, and I've had two years of music college. Martha was valedictorian of her class, and if she would stop to think before she speaks she could do as well as I. But Martha's thoughts are busy elsewhere," he finished with a smile.

Dave, pondering on the multitudinous tasks Martha

127

performed each day could well believe that English grammar had little room in her thoughts.

John's mornings were occupied with the care of the
half dozen buildings that comprised the block owned by
the hospital. He collected rents, supervised the work of
the boys who did the janitor work, and was responsible
for the maintenance of the buildings. These duties he dis-
charged conscientiously but with little zest. His real joy
in work lay in the music lessons with which every afternoon and many evenings were filled. Boys and girls,
young men and young women came to his door with
violin, trumpet or huge horn, or sat with John at piano
or harp in the large parlor across the hall from Dave's
room. All sorts of music came from that room, from the
painfully slow, jerky exercises of the littlest pianist to
the clear, high notes of the flutist whom John was preparing for the state high school contest.

Best of all was the music which came when John was
waiting for a pupil or enjoying a rare half hour alone.
Then a wondrous flood of such music poured out that
the listeners across the hall were lifted out of their pain
and care and borne along on the waves of melody. Listening, Dave forgot his weary body and JoAnne found her
heart lifted as she went about her household tasks. John
had a theme song and after every session with the mas-
ters he would close with a solo that they never tired of
hearing.

> My faith looks up to Thee,
> Thou Lamb of Calvary,
> Saviour Divine!
> Now hear me while I pray,

Take all my guilt away,
Oh, let me from this day
Be wholly Thine!

Long after the tones had died away, JoAnne would find herself humming or hear Dave's soft whistle as he worked at something on the table in front of him.

May Thy rich grace impart
Strength to my fainting heart,
My zeal inspire.
As Thou hast died for me,
Oh, may my love to Thee
Pure, warm and changeless be,
A living fire!

Chapter 20

DAVE WAS UP in his chair for most of the day now, and hope was high that he would regain the use of his limbs before the summer was over. Surely it would be so, with his improved health and with John's persistent rubbing. Dr. Herman came several times a week and when Dave remonstrated about the size of the bill that must be accumulating, he answered gruffly,

"Don't think about it, son. It all goes on that contractor's bill. If you hadn't grabbed that other guy he would have been killed. And the workmen are saying that if you hadn't yelled a dozen of them would have been under that shovel when it fell. The contractor is getting off easy. Don't you worry about him. Anyway, I was just passing and thought I'd stop."

Miss Moxon, also, was often "just passing," and would drop in to counsel with JoAnne and bring greetings from the store. These messages brought cheer to JoAnne. She had been genuinely lonesome for the friends with whom she had worked for years. But Dave did not respond and could not be drawn into any of the conversation about either the store or the church. Since leaving the hospital he had persistently refused to see anyone from either place. Even the minister, after several attempts to talk with him, decided that it was best to leave him alone.

"We can always pray," he said to the young people who felt hurt and depressed at the fact that they could not help their friend. "Just now Dave needs quiet and rest. We'll do our share by praying. God can work in His own way to bring the boy out of this valley. We'll just stand by."

The folks from the store were not so understanding, and Amy Moxon had a hard time making them realize that Dave would not see them. If he was recovering as well as reports claimed, why did he turn from them?

"I wish you'd let them come," said Amy to Dave one day when JoAnne had gone shopping and they two were alone. "They feel badly that you have shut them out."

"Not half as bad as they'd feel if I let them in," he answered shortly. "We've discussed that enough, Moxy. They're not coming in here to pity me and go away to gossip. I couldn't take it! I can keep JoAnne believing I'm perfectly happy lying here like a log, but *you* know I'm not, and I won't have those guys and gals staring at me."

"You don't have to," she said, distress written on her plain, middle-aged face. "But they love you, Dave, and any one of them would give you one of his legs if he could."

"I don't want anybody's legs. I wouldn't wish this mess onto my worst enemy. Also I don't want — and I don't intend to have — company. You and Doc are different. You save my sanity. But nix on the gang!"

Amy started to reply, then as JoAnne's step was heard

on the back porch she began a story of how the girls in the Steno department were planning a shower on Patsy Lewis who was to marry George Crews next month. Dave's face changed as if by magic, and when JoAnne came in he greeted her joyfully and went off into a hilarious account of an argument that Luther and Judson had held under his window, that spot being farthest removed from John's hearing.

"You should have heard them," he chuckled. "I assume that Luther teases Judson unmercifully for Jud argued, apparently in defense of himself, 'Go on, tell Daddy if you want to. But don't forget he told me if I had to be a worm, to remember that finally even a worm will turn.' To which Lute replied in a much aggrieved manner, 'That's all right, but when a worm turns it just wiggles and flops. It don't *never* bite and scratch!' I wish I could imitate them better. Even with all John's coaching they are still little chocolate drops in language."

As Amy Moxon climbed the steps to the street, she heard them laughing together and her eyes blurred with tears, so that she collided with Martha who was returning from a day at the hospital.

"Oh, Miss Moxon, I hope I didn' bump you all! I take up jus' too much sidewalk, but I can' seem to help it. You'll excuse me, please."

"It wasn't your fault, Martha," said the nurse shakily. "I wasn't watching where I was going. I just was thinking." She wiped a tear from the corner of her eye as she spoke.

"An' I can guess what you's thinkin'. You been visitin' my kids."

"Yes. They're my kids, too, Martha. Dave breaks my heart every time I'm with him. JoAnne is so utterly oblivious to the seriousness of their problem and Dave spends all his energies keeping her so. I wonder if she will ever grow up!"

"She better grow up," said Martha grimly. "I don' know why I don' spank her sometimes. But I jus' couldn' do it. She's so little an'— an' there's jus' somethin' about her —"

Miss Moxon laughed. "That's it. There's just something about her! And we all pamper and pet her, and hide the truth from her. Dave will never let her suspect what he is beginning to believe, and what you and I know. That boy will never walk again and she had better begin to face facts or —"

"Or God will step in and make her," Martha's tone had grown grim again. "I don't want to prophesy, Miss Moxon dear, but God may jus' have to shake that chil' awake."

"If He does, He'll do it in love, Martha. Don't forget that He loves her more than we do."

"He does, an' that's a comfort, sure nuff! I keep remindin' myse'f of that. If I fetch an' carry for her when my fingers itch to spank her instead, I don' need to fret that God'll get cross with her."

"No, He won't. I know how tenderly He can chastise when one of his weak children needs it. I don't fear to leave JoAnne in His hands."

"Tha's right. He even puts His arms under an' bears me up when the goin' is too much for my stren'th. He's a wonderful Lord, Miss Moxon, honey."

"He is, indeed, and He will see our youngsters through if we put them in His hands."

"Yes, ma'am. He sure nuff will!"

"So the days marched on. Martha and Amy Moxon prayed, JoAnne worked in the tiny kitchen cooking dishes that would tempt Dave's appetite and dreaming of the days when he should be able to be back at work. John rubbed and pounded the tired back and the useless limbs. Dave sat in his wheel chair by the window watching the people pass on the street above him or making up stories to tell JoAnne about what they would do when they moved to the little place out in the suburbs.

Spring changed into summer, and on a hot June night in the shabby old house on the back street, David Robertson, Junior, made his entrance into the world. JoAnne went very far down into the valley that night, and all that Miss Moxon and Dr. Herman could do seemed of no avail to bring her back to them. But Dave remembered the night at the hospital when she had called him back from the shadows, and it was his voice that finally recalled her to consciousness and the struggle to live. While doctor and nurse labored with her, Martha's capable hands dressed the baby and brought him to Dave as he sat in his chair. It was he who placed the baby on the pillow and leaned over to whisper to a white-faced JoAnne who was breathing regularly at last,

"Your son, Mrs. Robertson!"

Chapter 21

From the first Dave proved himself a capable nurse. He could get about the room in his chair as fast as JoAnne could walk, and he delighted in the care of his small son. He read all the books on child care that Miss Moxon and JoAnne could find for him, and he kept them all in a constant state of mirth with his original ideas on the subject. He kept careful notes of each new development or experience, declaring that he intended to write a book himself that would be the final authority on such matters.

They could not deny that he got good results, for Davie grew and flourished "like a green bay tree," as Martha expressed it. He was four months old and so heavy that JoAnne found him an uncomfortable load if she had to carry him, when the problem of finances became so acute that they held a consultation to decide what the next move should be.

"Perhaps I could get some work of some sort to do at home," said Dave, not very hopefully. "You could go get it and deliver it for me."

"Well, maybe. But you couldn't work amid so much

confusion as there is in these three little rooms."

"I could, because I'd have to. We must do something, keeda. Until an agreement is reached between Brantwell's and the construction company, we won't get any more compensation. If Dad were here it would have been settled at once. But I can't have any confidence that Slade is trying very hard. Anyway,— here we are. I don't want Doc or Moxy to know how we stand. But our bank account is melting like snow in July."

"Oh, I wish Dad were here! Hasn't anyone written him?"

"Not me. I never would. Doc says he's better but they have no assurance that he will ever be able to work again. No help from Dad, keeda. We have to work it out alone."

Dave had several plans and schemes for working at home, but none of them proved practicable, and the small bank account grew perilously slim.

One morning as JoAnne watched Dave bathe his son with the tub placed on a low bench beside his chair, she spoke hesitantly.

"Dave, I've been thinking."

"Good business! What's the answer?"

"I could go to work again."

"No!"

"But I could, dear, just for a little while, until you get started at something. Or better yet, you can concentrate on getting stronger. I *know* you'll be ready for new feet by spring. Let me work just this winter until you can take over again."

"Where would you work? Not at Brantwell's."

"No,—not if you don't want me to go there. But there are a lot of factories near here, and—"

"You're not going to work in a factory."

"It needn't be so bad. Lots of people do."

"Not you, keeda. You're not built for it."

"All factory work isn't heavy. Anyway, they ought to need typists in a factory as much as they do in a store."

"Well—O.K. A typist's job. But only for awhile until I can take over again."

JoAnne had turned away and did not see the hopeless pain in Dave's eyes nor the dispirited droop to his shoulders. To her, it was a happy solution to their difficulties. She did not like to leave the quiet of her home to enter into the world of business once more but it seemed the only thing to do, and it would last only a few months. By spring Dave would be back at Brantwell's and she would be at home caring for the baby.

A place was soon found in the office in a factory only fifteen minutes' ride from home, and the next week JoAnne found herself back in an office, while Dave kept the home fires burning. As she walked from the streetcar the first evening she found her thoughts turning backward to the days when she and Dave used to come home together to the other apartment.

"What a change in a year! We planned for me to stay at home while Dave went by leaps and bounds to the position of vice-president. And here we are in this ugly place and I'm working while Dave stays at home to wash dishes, take care of Davie and learn how to prepare our meals."

She smiled at a sudden thought. "He'll put his whole

heart into being a cook. Probably he will be publishing a cookbook by spring. Bless his heart! I'm glad he can be so happy over it all. I couldn't stand it if he were bitter or despondent. And oh, how glad I am that it's only temporary. I can live through the winter that's just ahead by thinking of the happy spring that's bound to follow it."

JoAnne was right in her prediction. Dave attacked the problems of home-making with zest and earnestness. With the same determination which had made him an excellent nurse for the baby, he went at the housekeeping and cooking. Following JoAnne's careful instructions he learned to cook their simple meals, and it was a source of great pride to him to have an appetizing meal ready when she came home at night. As they ate, they recounted the day's doings, JoAnne introducing Dave to her new acquaintances in the office of the box factory, and he regaling her with stories of the happenings among the music students who came and went across the hall, or the bickerings, good-natured or otherwise, among Martha's and John's numerous progeny. The doors between the apartment and John's studio were left open so that Dave could feel at all times the availability of John's strong arms and back, hence the sayings and doings of the Moseby family filled Dave's days with interest.

"I'm thinking of writing a book," he announced one evening. But before he could proceed, JoAnne's laugh interrupted.

"I knew it! I told myself you'd do it. I know all about it. It will be a cookbook!"

"Say! That's one I hadn't thought of. Thanks for the idea. But that one will take a long time. I'd want the recipes to be original ones so it will require a long period of 'trial and error' effort. But this book can be started any time. Martha's and 'Jawn's' boys and girls will be my characters. I've been trying to learn their names and I think I have them all. Do you know them?"

"I should say not! I can't even tell which ones of the mob belong here."

"Well, I can, now. Just you listen. Luther is the oldest. He is in eighth grade and is decidedly anti-social. I suspect he's a genius of some sort. Judson is next. He's an imp, and his personality clashes with Luther's forty times a day. Moody comes next. He's—"

JoAnne giggled. "Is the next one named Billy Sunday?"

"No. The next one is Mary Slessor. Do you know anyone by that name?"

"No. Who was she?"

"A missionary to Africa. Mary told me so, herself. She intends to follow in the footsteps of her namesake. Then comes Ann Hasseltine. After that is Samjones — that's all one name — and the baby's name is —"

"Sissy!" said JoAnne. "I've heard that often enough to know it."

"Wrong! That's her *nom de plume*. Her name is Narcissa."

"What! No minister or missionary? Martha must be backsliding."

"So I thought, but Mary enlightened me. Cissy spells her name with a C. She is Narcissa Whitman, martyred missionary to the Indians. That's all of them. If I could put them on paper, catch their personalities, picture them so that a reader could see them as I see them all day long, it would be a best seller."

"Put in Martha too. They wouldn't be what they are without her hand on the wheel."

"Right you are. And her 'Jawn' will have to be there, too. He's not as evident at all times as she is, but I've an idea he's the real captain of the ship."

"That's the way it should be. The men are the captains. We women are first mates. Sometimes we forget and take over, but we don't really mean it. We like to be bossed."

"H'm. *That* will take a bit of proving."

"Anyway, it ought to be a good book."

"There's material in this house for several. There's the Katzes on the second floor. They are both working and saving their money so that they can bring some relatives over from Germany. They don't carry home enough groceries to keep a cat well fed, and they look hungry all the time."

"I'd like to meet them. They sound nice."

"Maybe you could take them some cookies next time you bake. Then in the other apartment above us are the Polowskys. They are dark and glum and unfriendly. Lute thinks they are counterfeiters because they carry out mysterious packages every week. But I suspect some finished work of some kind,— something they bring home to do evenings. Mary says Mr. Polowsky has only two pairs of socks. She knows, because Mrs. P. washes them each day and hangs them on the back stair railing. And every other day the same pair appears."

"There's a third floor room, isn't there?"

142

"Yes. A faded southern belle lives there. She sings. She doesn't go to work until noon, and all morning she warbles. Some of the songs would wring your heart. How's this?

> In a little rosewood casket that is resting on the stand
> Is a package of old letters written by a loving hand.
> Go and get them for me, sister, read them over all to me.
> I have often tried to read them but for tears I could not see.

There's four more verses each one sadder than the last, and by the time she's sung them all we are both ready to cry. She's a good scout, though. She is always giving Martha's girls some little gift, and she is teaching Mary to sew."

"I like her. What's her name?"

"Miss Melton. Mabelle Melton. I heard her tell Jawn. She takes piano lessons from him. That's when I heard her sing. If she has to wait for Jawn she gives me a concert."

Listening to his chatter, JoAnne felt her heart lifted up. As long as Dave was happy and confident, all was well with her life. During the time last winter when Dave's life had hung in the balance in the hospital she had been sure that if he died she could not continue to live. She understood, as even Dave did not, that it was his love and care that kept back the fear and panic of her black moods. It had seemed to her then that they were there in the shadows all the time just waiting to see if Dave were going to die. When he got better they drew back, and now with Dave getting well and with Davie so rosy and sweet there were no shadows where such terrors could hide. So she worked as hard as she could in the office and went happily home each evening to her waiting boys.

As for Dave, so long as he could keep JoAnne happy and prevent her from discovering the depths of despair to which he sometimes descended on those lonely days, he counted himself successful. Were it not for her need of him he would be sorry that she called him back to life that night when he almost slipped away. For as the weeks and months passed he realized that Dr. Herman was becoming increasingly discouraged about the paralyzed limbs. With this realization came the utter abandonment of his own hope. All of John's patient work had been of no avail. There was no more life in his legs now than there had been the day they brought him home. And there never would be.

Some day, of course, JoAnne would have to know. But he would keep it from her as long as he could. As time went on she would grow so used to seeing him thus, that when her gradual awareness of the truth became knowledge it might be easier for her than if he tried to tell her now. Until he could find some way in which he could earn a living for his family JoAnne must keep on at the box factory. To enable her to do this he must allow no hint of discouragement or foreboding to communicate itself to her. So he laughed and teased, boasted of his cooking, talked of the books he was going to write, and in every way tried to appear to have not a care in the world.

The breakfast table devotions that JoAnne had shared, first with Nona then with Dave, went on as usual. If JoAnne noticed that Dave chose to read the Scripture each morning and leave the praying to her it did not seem significant. No matter which one of them prayed aloud, both were praying in their hearts, she mused. Her heart was so tender and full of love for him that whatever he desired was all right with her. He seemed happy, therefore she was happy.

So Dave went through his valley alone, and fought the powers of darkness singlehanded. Then, with no signs of the battle to betray him, he managed to make JoAnne's hours at home times of joyous fellowship.

Chapter 22

It was a rainy morning. The clouds hung so low that at eight o'clock when JoAnne tied on her scarf the tiny bedroom was dark and gloomy. She did not like the weather. She had a cold and she felt chilled at the thought of going out into the rain. Her face was sober as he kissed Davie good-by, and she gave no answering smile to Dave's tender, "Good-by, honey. Please be careful."

As she trudged along the street she had to walk carefully to avoid the puddles for the sidewalks were broken and treacherous.

"A grand neighborhood we live in!" she complained mentally. "And a mess of a day to be out. I wonder how it would feel to stay in a nice warm, dry home all day, — to be able to cook and play with Davie and really live. Davie hardly knows me. I'm just his provider. Dave is his parent."

She reached the corner just in time to see a car pull away. No other was in sight and she huddled under her umbrella feeling utterly miserable. Her whole life seemed as dreary as the ugly district about her. Was she going to have to work all summer? Here it was almost spring, and Dave wasn't better. Was he trying as hard as he could? Or had he grown to like this way of living? Maybe it was all in his mind. She had heard of folks being that way.

The car was coming and she felt in her bag for her coin purse. It was not there, and she realized with a start of dismay that she had left it on her dresser. The knowledge that she must return through the mud and drizzle to get it added the last straw to her load. Four extra blocks! And her feet were already wet and her hands cold. Oh, if only she could stay at home today!

She ran through the alley and up the walk to the back door. It opened noiselessly, and she had stepped into the kitchen before she heard Dave's voice from the living room. She stood still, — listening, her face pale with shock. It *couldn't* be Dave speaking so. And yet it *was* Dave. His voice came clearly and the words she heard made JoAnne feel sick and weak.

"It's all rot, John, — I tell you it's all rot! Any kind of a decent God wouldn't let a guy down like He's let *me* down!"

"He's not let you down, boy. He's trying to lift you up."

"If He were really God, He could do it without this day-by-day slow torture He's feeding me. I'm done with Him, John, and you needn't preach at me. If I weren't such a helpless log I'd get out in front of one of those trucks and end it all."

"Now, now, boy, just go easy. Let me work on this

other leg awhile. Seems to me it feels more alive this morning."

"That's just another lie. It's dead and you know it! Maybe you can all fool JoAnne, but not me. I'm dead from the waist down and they ought to bury me. Then JoAnne could get a *real* man!"

She had stopped in the middle of the kitchen, just out of sight from the bed where John was working. She had remained quiet, trying to comprehend that this hysterical outburst really came from Dave. At these last words she started forward but the voice stopped her again.

"Some folks say there's no hell, John. But there is. I can tell them so. I can describe it to them. It's lying here realizing I can't even get out of bed until you come to help me. It's looking at that dead rat that's hanging out of that rainspout next door and that scenic wonder of garbage cans out there. It's cooking and baby-tending when I want to be doing a man's work. It's just hell, John. Look at this other window. What do I see all day long? Just feet! Other people's feet that can walk and run. Do you know where my feet are, John? They're buried where the rest of me ought to be!"

John's voice answered as Dave stopped for breath. "You aren't talking sense, Dave, and you know it. God hasn't let you down, but you're sure letting Him down. If you'd only — "

"Well, I won't. I'm done with Him. If all power belongs to Him, He could have saved my feet and legs.

149

I hadn't turned my back on Him. He's turned against me. He must like to torture!"

"Dave! Stop right there! You can't — "

"Oh, yes, I can! And you needn't quote Scripture to me. I can do some quoting myself. Listen to this. I was reading it yesterday. It was another David crying out to God. And what did he get? 'All thy waves and thy billows have gone over me.' That's what He's done to me, John, and it's black, and deep, — and awful!"

As JoAnne listened it seemed that the shadows of the day grew deeper. The rain outside made a dirge on the roof. All the fear and horror that had been kept down and almost forgotten, crowded around her again. If Dave were afraid — if Dave had lost his hope and the joy of living, what could she do? She felt the approach of the old panic and there was in her no will to fight it. She knew that she should not scream, but she could not control the hysteria that was mounting in her. And there was no one to help her. Nona was gone and Dave was gone!

She was standing in the middle of the floor, staring at the doorway through which she could see John's back as he methodically rubbed. She tried to summon strength to turn and tiptoe from the room, but she could not move. All resistance was gone and she opened her mouth to scream with the terror that held her. But before a sound had come a large black hand came over her open lips with a pressure so firm that sound was impossible, and she was lifted in a strong arm, carried across the porch and set down in Martha's kitchen. As she stood there, before Martha could close the door she

150

heard Dave cry, "Oh, God, never to see another sunrise on the beach!"

Martha released her and uttered a stern admonition, "Up them stairs, young lady, and don't you yell one little yelp, or I'll spank you. I been wantin' to a long time."

In a daze JoAnne stumbled up the steep stairs and was led by Martha into a plainly furnished bedroom. Hardly knowing what she did she let her shoes be removed and her coat and scarf taken from her.

"Now you lay down here awhile. I'm goin' down to make you some tea, an' if you yell while I'm gone I'll tan you!"

JoAnne knew that she meant it, and anyway she didn't feel like screaming now. She was too tired. She lay back on the pillow but she could not rest. She was shaking with a chill, and her heart felt as big as her whole body and heavy as lead. Martha returned with the tea and through chattering teeth she drank it. Martha put a hot water bottle at her feet and tucked a heavy blanket around her.

"You can't afford a col'," she scolded. "You gonna lay here an' rest awhile an' warm up till you quits that chatterin'."

"I — I — have to go to work."

"No work for you today. I telephone' while the water was heatin'. You gotta lay here an' get quiet an' build up gumption enough to go back to that boy tonight an' face him with a smile."

"I can't! Oh, Martha, I never can!"

"Yes, you can an' you will! You're a grown-up woman,

an' you gonna act like one." JoAnne lay still and Martha's relentless voice went on. "This thing's been buildin' up for months, maybe years. As I sense it, you never have faced life straight front like you'd ought. You're always hidin' behin' somebody else, an' that boy downstairs has had you aroun' his neck even with his poor broke back hol'in' him down. He's stood about all he can stan'. Now he's crackin' under the load an' it's up to you to do some growin' up so's you can walk alone."

"I can't go alone! It frightens me!"

"Well, if you don' stiffen up that spaghetti backbone of yours, you're gonna be really alone for the res' of your life."

JoAnne lay with closed eyes, looking so white and weak that Martha's tender heart ached for her. She was such a little thing and life had dealt her some very stiff blows. But this was not the time for Martha to weaken, so, although her tone softened a bit, she continued to admonish.

"Whatever made you such a 'fraidcat, anyhow? God never meant anybody to be like that."

By direct questions and subtle proddings she finally broke through JoAnne's reserve, and the whole story came out. The halting words told more than just the bare incidents of a frail young mother who had to leave her child, an adopted sister who gave her own life to care for the timid girl, and a devoted lad who loved her too much to demand strength from her. The sensitive soul of Martha read into the recital the terrors and fancies that were not put into words, and tears of sympathy filled the brown eyes.

When the story was ended, JoAnne turned wearily on the pillow and lay quiet and hopeless. Martha tucked the blanket again about the girl's shoulders, then rubbing with one strong black hand the white forehead where the veins throbbed too rapidly, began to sing.

"Don' yo' cry, ma honey!
Don' you' weep no mo'.
Mammy's gwine hol' her chile, her baby!"

It seemed to JoAnne that she really was held in arms that were all-sufficient for her need and weakness. Her tense nerves began to relax. The soft tones were soothing and brought a sense of peace. As Martha drifted from her lullaby into a hymn, JoAnne sank into sleep.

When she awakened the sun was shining into the west window. She looked in bewilderment at Amy Moxon sitting by her side busy with some knitting. As she moved the nurse looked up with a smile.

"Well, little girl, feel better?"

"Yes. I must have slept a long time. What are you doing here?"

"Martha called me after lunch when she knew you'd be waking up."

"I don't know why I slept so long."

"I do. Martha made some of her famous 'yarbs.'"

JoAnne smiled wryly. "That's nothing to the punch she put in the tongue-lashing she gave me."

"Bless her heart! She has shed many tears today over having done it. Martha is the original 'it-hurts-me-worse-than-it-hurts-you' mother. But she does her duty by her children, anyway. Her children get their share of paddling."

"I got my share this morning."

"Yes, you did, and I'm afraid you needed it. Something has to be done, and done quickly, dear, if we're
going to pull Dave through this slump and help him
get hold of himself."

"I didn't know he had sl-slumped!"

"No, you didn't because he had determined that you
shouldn't. At first the effort he made to keep cheerful
before you was beneficial to him. But it has gone too far.
He's on the verge of complete nervous collapse now.
Something *has* to be done and you're the only one that
can do it."

"Oh, no! I can't do anything!"

"You must, and you can. You took hold like a
real soldier that first night in the hospital. The need is
as great now."

"But *how* can I do anything?"

"First, you have to go back and ignore the fact that
you ever heard a thing this morning. Dave thinks you've
been at work all day and you need not let him know
otherwise. Instead of feeling sorry for yourself and
letting Dave cheer you up, you are going to be so gay
tonight that he can relax from the pressure of holding
you up. Can you do it?"

"I don't — see how."

"Just keep reminding yourself that it's for Dave. He'd
die for you, JoAnne. Can't you do this for him?"

JoAnne drew a long breath. "I'll try."

"You'll do more than try. You'll *do* it. You've got a
real job ahead of you, dear, but I've faith to believe you

154

can put it across. In these next weeks you must convince Dave without putting it into words that you are strong enough to bear the knowledge that he will never walk again, and — "

"Oh, no! No!"

"Hush, dear. Yes, you might as well face it. We have all hoped and believed otherwise, but now we must accept the truth. Dr. Herman says there is no sign of life in those poor limbs."

JoAnne moaned as the bitter blow struck her. Amy blinked back her tears and continued to rub the limp hands. After a few minutes she continued resolutely,

"You had to know it, dear, and now you have to face it, and accept it, and help Dave to turn it into a blessing."

"Is that possible?"

"You are a wife and mother, and today you must grow up to it. You must put your hand in Dave's and the two of you together can go through your valley of Baca and make a well there."

"What does *that* mean?"

"Baca means 'bitter.' Oh, that Eighty-fourth Psalm! Read it as soon as you can, honey. If the waters of the valley are bitter, the Christian who must pass through it, — and we all have our valleys, JoAnne — can have a well of ever springing, clear, sweet water that will refresh and strengthen. And the one who has found a well in the valley will always have water to pass on to other weary ones."

JoAnne lay quietly, looking at the gray head bent over the knitting. Amy's face was plain, but there was a sweetness about her that drew to her care all the needy ones she met. Had Amy had her valley and come through it with a great supply of refreshing for others? Is that why she was always so full of strength when she was needed? And what about Martha? Did the sadness in the brown eyes and the peace on her face mean that she, too, had found the ever springing fountain sufficient? Then, unbidden, the memory of Nona's face on that last night came before JoAnne; and she knew why it was that Nona could go with a smile, understanding that she would never come back. She drew a long breath and spoke slowly.

"It will be hard."

"Of course it will. And you can't do it alone. But there is One who will enable. He went through His valley alone, and gave His life for you. He will not desert you now. Lean hard on Him and He will bear you up."

"I will do my best to do what you say tonight. But what comes after that?"

"Take it one step at a time. Let God lead the way. Keep the thought before you that you must be the strong one for awhile, and show such love to Dave and faith in God that your places will be reversed. Dave will lean on you for a change. Let him know that in spite of his condition you still need him and that you love him more than all the rest of the world."

"Oh, I do! Even more than Davie!"

"That's as it should be, dear. Now I can't tell you any more. You'll have to go on without me or Martha. God will have to chart your course."

As JoAnne was silent the nurse slipped to her knees

beside the bed and prayed aloud. It reminded JoAnne of the time Martha had prayed with her in the hospital. This time, however, when the prayer had ended she herself sent up a petition.

"Dear God, I'm so frightened and tired and ashamed that I don't know how to do the things I have to do. Help me to help Dave and teach us both how to trust Thee more. Show us how Thy way is best even though it does go through the valley. Help us to train Davie for Thee. Thank Thee for Martha and Jawn and a friend like Amy Moxon. Bless her for Jesus' sake. Amen."

They arose from their knees and Amy wiped her eyes. But JoAnne resolutely picked up her shoes and began to put them on.

"The first thing is to go out and do the shopping and arrive home at five-thirty as usual. I can take that step all right. I'll take the second step when I get there."

Chapter 23

IN LATER YEARS when JoAnne looked back on the months that followed that day they were, in her memory, a chaotic jumble of determined effort, occasional signs of success, all too frequent feelings of defeat, and constant stumbling, falling, and "rising to fight better." From the viewpoint of those later years, the road showed an upward climb, even though there were small dips in the path that told of temporary loss of ground. But as she lived through it, taking one day at a time, she often felt that she was failing in her task.

The first evening was not so difficult. On the impetus of the high resolves she had made, and aided by Amy who had announced herself as an uninvited supper guest, she was able to be really gay. Dave, too, seemed unusually elated. He had prepared a new casserole dish and openly complimented himself on the achievement. Davie's first tooth had chosen this day to appear and that called for a celebration.

"You don't know how relieved we are, old fellow," Dave informed him. "We had just about decided to get you some false ones."

John was having a final practice with a string quartette that was to be in a concert the next night, and they drew their chairs in front of the door and enjoyed the music.

"I've paid good dollars for a less comfortable seat and music that couldn't hold a candle to this," Amy said in relaxed appreciation.

When it was time for her to leave, she stood for a moment after she had put on her wraps and looked at them. Then she spoke abruptly.

"It makes me homesick to visit you youngsters. My own folks all live so far away that I feel like an orphan. I want to thank you for a lovely evening. Can't we pray together before I leave?"

She herself did most of the praying, but JoAnne in a steady voice added a few sentences. When she asked, "Please give us strength for whatever Thou hast purposed for us," Dave's hand, lying over hers, tightened convulsively on it. But his voice, too, was calm when he closed with a firm "Amen." After Miss Moxon had gone, John came in to prepare Dave for bed, and JoAnne had time only for a quick kiss before she left him.

Perhaps it was that prayer of hers which planted in his mind the seed of belief that she might develop more strength. For, as she began, in small ways, to lean on him less, he responded by appearing to expect more from her. The first time this was noticeable was on a night when a sudden thunderstorm had arisen. Dave remembered other nights when she had cowered in his arms at each flash or clap. Tonight she went calmly on with her ironing, and if her hands shook and her face had

160

lost its color Dave did not mention it. After the storm had passed and a wan moon was peeping from behind the clouds he called for her.

"Keeda, come and look at the sky."

She stood beside his chair, gazing at the scurrying clouds and the pale moon, and said.

"Storms always end, don't they, Dave?"

Her hands as they lay on his shoulders were still trembling, but her voice was quiet.

The next step she took was in watching John rub Dave's limbs. She had always left the room when this was done, for the sight of his helplessness sickened her. In the daytime in his chair he seemed alive, and she occasionally forgot his terrible handicap. But when he was lifted in John's arms and laid on the bed his inert figure shocked her. As Dave lay on his back he was accustomed to keep one arm flung across his eyes as if to shut out the sight of John's efforts. So he did not see JoAnne on this night as she stood in the doorway watching them. For a moment only she stood there, her lips moving silently, then she came noiselessly across the floor to stand by the bedside. As the deliberate massaging continued, she watched John's strong hands in their tireless task then spoke casually with no hint of the trepidation she had to fight down.

"My hands aren't as big as yours, Jawn, but if you'd teach me I could learn how to do that."

John did not answer, and it was several minutes before Dave said anything. Then his casual tone matched hers.

"I think she could, at that, Jawn. She has a mighty clever pair of hands."

"I *know* I can. I'll watch for several days, then I'll practice and Jawn can see how I do and correct me if I go wrong."

She did this, and several times under John's supervision she took over the last fifteen minutes.

"She's so little that a person with good nerves and muscles couldn't feel it," John said to Martha. "But it does her good to try it, and it does him good to know that she wants to. She can't hurt him, and if she doesn't help him — well, neither do I."

John was right. Physically it made no difference in Dave's condition, but little by little he was realizing the growth in JoAnne and letting himself relax in her presence. As the days went by, there grew between them a closeness that they had not known in the carefree moments of the races along the beach. As yet, it was an intangible thing of which they could not speak, but it was there and JoAnne was sure that it could be nurtured into stronger life. Someday they would be able to discuss their Baca together and drink from its well!

Chapter 24

On a stifling night in early June, sleep would not come to JoAnne in the little room where her bed and Davie's crib were crowded close together. It had been a tiring day followed by an evening made nerve-racking by the clamor from the back yard where Martha's noisy brood played Cops and Robbers with the little Gallios, Goldbergs, Cohens and Kalinskis of the neighborhood. Their raucous screams and laughter had cut across her tired nerves like the lashes of a whip. Davie had been cross, and Dave morose and silent. She wondered if there had been any real gain in their attitudes, or if they had slumped back to the old discouragement and despair.

Now as she lay, not daring to stir lest she waken Davie, there came to her a picture of an attic room where a young mother lay beside a frightened child and tried to soothe her. This picture had come to her several times in her life, and she had become convinced that it was a memory of the mother she had lost. Now she felt her heart go out in sympathy to that mother. She must have carried intolerable burdens and she must

163

have prayed for her baby. That would be why there had always been a hand to help when she needed it, — Nona, Dave, Mr. Brantwell, Amy Moxon, Martha and John. But tonight none of them was here and she was too tired and discouraged to go on. She thought of the baby girl nestling in the curve of a shielding arm, and wished with all her heart that she might forget about being strong and brave and could just let go and let someone else hold her up. If Dave were only awake she might creep to his side and let his strong arm hold her while she cried out her weariness on his shoulder.

How unbearably hot it was! No breeze came through the small window and the air was heavy and humid. She found it difficult to breathe in the oppressive atmosphere. She lay with closed lids while scalding tears ran onto the pillow.

A sound from the other room startled her. Was Dave also awake? She had thought him asleep long before she came to bed. Perhaps he had wakened and wanted a drink of water. She started to rise, then as she caught the sound more clearly she fell back again on the pillow and lay as if stricken. Dave was crying in the night!

At first she felt only dismay and fright. Did he do this often? It would be terrible to see Dave cry. She remembered that morning when she had stood in the kitchen and heard him crying out against God. She had never let him discover that he had been overheard. Maybe that was what she must do now, — just lie still, and presently he would go to sleep. In the morning he would be all right and need never know that she had been awake.

But minute after minute ticked by on the clock on the dresser, and still those terrible smothered sobs continued. She *must* go to him. At the thought she felt a rush of panic, — the old fear that used to send her screaming to Nona's or Dave's arms. What good would it do for her to try to help Dave when she might start screaming herself? And yet she *had* to do something. She couldn't let those sobs go on and on. She sent up a prayer for help and started across the floor. He was lying on his back with his arms across his eyes like a heartbroken small boy. The sight of him made her forget her own fears and she was across the floor and by his side before he realized her presence. Seating herself on the bed, without a word she drew him into her arms. At her touch the barriers were downed and he sobbed unrestrainedly, clinging to her with frantic appeal. She sat in silence until he quieted somewhat, then she began to sing softly. She could feel his arms loosen as he relaxed and grew quiet. There were several shuddering sobs, and at last a half chuckle as he said,

"You're an angel, keeda, but you're off-key as usual."

She laughed shakily, then arose, closed the bedroom door and turned on the light.

"I'm going to get the alcohol and give you a cool rub. And I'm going to talk while I do it."

"Am I going to get a scolding?" he asked shamefacedly.

"Well, — I think not tonight. I'm just going to pass on to you some of the wonderful things I've been finding out. I guess that as a Christian I've been pretty immature, Dave. But Amy has been helping, and so has Martha. They know so much that I have never thought of. And they've been awfully good to try to teach me. I'd like to share some of it with you."

So as she rubbed she talked, haltingly and with some confusion, for she had never tried to put such thoughts into words before. She told of the valley of bitterness, of its arid desert, its rocky paths, its sharp stones that cut and tore, and of the thirst of the travelers who passed that way. Then she told of One who was there to give living water to all who would accept it that they might find blessing even in Baca.

"That's what Christ has done for me lately, Dave. He's given me fresh water in place of the bitterness, and He's made me able to do the things I thought I couldn't possibly do. He's even made me love to do them. He's made it a time of blessing. And He can do the same for you. We can't go around our valley, dear. We have to go through it. But there's lots of fresh water in it and at the end — " her voice broke but she went on, "at the end will be a wonderful place where Nona will be, — and our mothers, — and your dad. Jesus will be there, and we'll all walk and talk with Him. We can take the valley if we know that He will lead us out into such a place. We can do it together, can't we?"

His answer was slow in coming. "I — I — don't mind it so much for myself, sweetheart. But what it has done to you breaks my heart!"

"And I don't mind it for myself, Dave. I just long to make you happy."

"Don't you get tired of the everlasting grind? I had such big plans for taking care of you, and here I am, — just a useless lump!"

"Listen, dear. If I could make you well I'd give my life to do it. But I can't. Even this way, though, I wouldn't trade places with *anybody*. Dave, you're so dear to me that I feel like the richest woman on earth at this minute. Being yours and knowing that you are mine makes me just full of happiness!"

She drew him close again and their lips met in a kiss that meant more than any other kiss had ever meant to them. She went on with the rubbing and they were silent until he seized one of her hands and said sleepily,

"Your hands are little but potent. You've given me something that Jawn never could give. Run along to sleep, keeda. I can rest now. I feel like my mother had rocked me to sleep."

She had thought that she could not sleep in the stifling bedroom, but her heart was so full of peace and joy that the heat went unnoticed and almost as soon as her head touched the pillow she slept. Her last waking thought was,

"It's true what I said to Dave. We *can* do it together."

Day after day, hot days and hard ones, sunny days and cloudy ones, they traveled on. Sometimes they seemed to go swiftly as if borne on wings. Then there would be times when the hot sands of the valley were almost too much for them, and their strength seemed unequal to the journey's demands. There would be days at a stretch when Dave was gay and the little apartment rang with their fun. Then there would be times

167

of despondency when not even Davie's cunning tricks could bring a smile to his face. But the well was always there and JoAnne drank deeply, gaining strength that she could pass on to Dave. When she noticed with her newborn awareness that he did not partake for himself, she said nothing. Ever before her was the memory of his hysterical disavowal of faith in a God who would permit the pounding blows that laid men low. He had not yet given any sign that his attitude had changed. His spirits had lifted so that he was more willing to try to fill in the long hours of the day with some books or games, or in listening to the radio. And when JoAnne came home, his happiness was not the simulated light-heartedness he had formerly assumed. But it was clear to all of them that his spiritual refreshing and his renewed courage came from JoAnne rather than from the real Source of strength.

The knowledge that she was able to help him was a strong stimulant to JoAnne's own morale. For the first time in her life she was giving rather than receiving help. Amy Moxon, watching them on her frequent visits, reported back to Dr. Herman.

"The whole atmosphere has changed. Dave still has his bad days, but he isn't afraid to show it now. There's none of that supercharged tension that made you fear an atomic explosion all the time. When he grouches he grouches and doesn't try to fool anybody. And JoAnne can usually bring him out of it in a short time."

"That's good news," grunted the doctor. "He's relaxed, and that's what I've been wanting. It's our only hope."

Chapter 25

IT WAS LUTHER and Judson, John's and Martha's two oldest sons, who were responsible for giving Dave a new interest in life and showing him that the traits which had made him Dad Brantwell's valuable assistant were still with him. It had been his keen understanding of human nature and his quick intuitive judgment of personnel problems that had appealed to the old man. Coupled with this was a real interest in even the humblest worker, and Dad had learned that when Dave solved a case there would be no complaints of injustice or misunderstanding.

All this was now in the past and Dave did not let his thoughts dwell on it. But as he began to take more interest in things outside his own room, it was impossible for the old instincts not to be stirred. On clear afternoons John pushed the chair into the back yard, and under the shade of a big box elder tree, Dave would sit and watch the comings and goings of the neighborhood, while Davie toddled about the playpen near by.

He soon learned the names and dispositions of each one of the mob of children that played through the yard and alley. Martha's youngsters were always in the midst of whatever projects were afoot. There was the usual amount of difference of opinions and childish quarrels, with the fierce arguments and quick reconciliations. But in one quarter Dave soon sensed real trouble. Between Lute and Jud a perpetual feud existed in spite of parental commands and discipline. Whenever they were together there would ensue bickering and argumentation that all too frequently ended in blows being struck. The neighborhood children had grown to expect a free show several times a week, and all that was needed to bring a crowd together was for the word to go forth, "Come on down the alley. Lute and Jud's fightin' again!"

Dave was mildly amused by these battlings, and chuckled to himself as he listened to their controversy. One day, however, he saw it in a different light. Martha, who had worked all night at the hospital and was trying to rest in her bedroom, had been aroused by an unusually noisy battle and came down to separate the belligerents and send them into separate rooms for an hour of enforced quiet. As she turned to go back into the house, Dave caught a glimpse of her face, and saw to his astonishment that tears were streaming down the brown cheeks, while the weary shoulders drooped with discouragement. With a rush of shame he realized that what had been amusing to him in the boys' differences, was tragic to John and Martha.

"Poor Martha!" he mused. "She loves both of them and has tried so desperately to get them to at least live in peace with each other. How would I feel if Davie had a brother and they hated each other like Jud and Lute do? I'd like to know what makes them act that way."

His interest, having been aroused, did not die, and he began to study the boys and their behavior. Whereas, heretofore, he had sat quietly reading or watching Davie, now he tried to attract the boys to gather around him where he could watch and listen. He taught them games he had played in the small town where he had been raised. His capable fingers helped with airplanes, puzzles, bird houses or whatever was the project of the moment. He directed treasure hunts, refereed ball games and whittled innumerable keepsakes from the scraps of wood they brought him. He told stories of Captain Kidd and Long John Silver. Little by little he grew to know all the children of the neighborhood. Many parents would have been surprised at the accurate character analysis Dave could have given of their children.

Especially did he study Luther and Judson, trying to discover the causes of such an unnatural situation. And one night he spoke to John while that patient chap rubbed and pounded the unreponsive limbs.

"Jawn, I think I have the key to the trouble between those two boys of yours."

John drew a long breath and let his hands rest idly on Dave's back. "Well, if you know that, you're a Solomon. Martha and I have tried for ten years to figure it out."

"Ten years? That would make it about the time Jud began to walk and talk."

"Yes, that's about when it started. What is it, Dave?"

171

"Jealousy."

"Jealousy? Who's jealous of whom?"

"Lute's jealous of Jud."

"But why?" asked John, beginning to knead the back muscles once more. "Lute's the oldest and gets some things Jud can't have. He's the smartest of all our youngsters and has more talent. He has nothing to be jealous about."

"He thinks he has. And he tries to get back at Jud by sharp digs and jibes. He can think of more ways to tease Jud than you would dream possible. Jud is a guileless kid and doesn't know what it's all about. But he has a hot temper and when he gets tired of being the butt of Lute's taunts the fight begins."

"That's the first thing you've said that makes sense, Dave. I know that's true. The fight begins, — yes, it always does. We're pretty sick of heart over it, Martha and I. We just can't figure it out. I guess we will just have to leave them in the Lord's hands."

"Look here, Jawn," said Dave with more animation in his voice than any of them had heard in all the months since he came into the old house. "I don't believe the Lord wants you to leave things with Him that you ought to take care of yourself. You ought to watch those kids like I've been doing. Jud is a happy, friendly chap and every kid in the block loves him. He's in on everything that goes on. When they choose sides everybody wants Jud. He doesn't know half as many things as Lute does, but he has a natural talent for friendliness. The kids don't care for the things that Lute knows. To them he is just a slowpoke who can't run as fast or throw as far or laugh at nothing as easily as Jud does. Lute resents Jud's popularity and strikes out with the only weapon he has, — his tongue. He is already an adept at stinging, biting wit, — the kind that inflicts a real wound. His tongue trips Jud's hair-trigger temper and then the fur begins to fly."

"Sounds logical, Dave. Jud *is* a good-natured fellow, and I know everybody likes him better than Lute. But I didn't know that Lute cared. He doesn't act as if he wants friends."

"Sure, he doesn't. He's too sensitive to let you know how he feels. But if ever I saw a boy who's hungry for a lot of loving, it's Luther."

John worked away without saying anything for several minutes. When he spoked his voice was rough with feeling.

"That's a rebuke to me, Dave. Lute is mighty dear to me. Of course, all my kids are. But he's my oldest, — and — and, — well, what do you think we ought to do?"

"I don't know that, Jawn. But we'll work on it."

"We'll do more than that. We'll pray on it."

"You do the praying, and I'll work on it. Do I have your permission?"

"You sure do. And Martha and I will remember to let him know he means something special to us. He was so little when he got pushed off our laps by others that he's never had his share, I guess. Thank you, Dave, for opening my eyes. I surely do appreciate the interest you're taking in my boys."

Dave worked day after day with the boys, winning

their confidence, teaching them the principles of good sportsmanship and trying to develop in them some fraternal love and loyalty. It was a slow process, and the backslidings seemed more frequent than the forward movements. There were days when Dave thought he had taken on a hopeless task. But there were other times when he dared to hope that he was achieving results. Martha and John, true to their promise, took more time for their boys. To Jud this made little difference. He loved everyone and took it for granted that they all returned the feeling. So when John drew him to his side and gave him an affectionate squeeze, Jud just gave a happy grin and scampered off to his play. But a similar demonstration brought self-conscious confusion to Lute. He eyed his father warily as if wondering what price was to be exacted for the gift. Having been awakened to the situation, however, John gave it his full backing and attention, and patiently went on about the business of winning the boy back to a state of trust.

By the end of the summer, there was a real improvement. Dave had won the boys to the point where he could talk frankly to them, and he had a long session with each.

"I hope the change is permanent," he said to JoAnne and Amy Moxon one evening as they observed them playing together. "It makes me sick to see what ill results can come from such small difficulties. I think every boy could be made into a good man by a little understanding at the right time."

"Did it ever occur to you, Dave," questioned Amy, "that you're done the biggest personnel job of your life, right here in your own back yard? And if you could do it here on a pair of naughty boys, you could handle Brantwell's problems. Some way could be found, I'm sure. And oh, how they need you these days!"

There was silence for many moments. JoAnne held her hands clenched in her lap, and did not dare to look at Dave. Would this make him angry? Then he spoke quietly, with no hint of what he might think of Amy's suggestion.

"I think I'd better wait awhile before I pronounce my patients cured." For from the alley came the sound of Lute and Jud in an argument! It ended without a fight however, and Dave gave a relieved sigh.

It was Martha who brought about the completion of the process of reconciliation. One morning as JoAnne went to work she met Martha and the two boys at the gate, loaded with bags, boxes, and quite bit of sport equipment.

"We're going on a picnic," Martha explained. "Some other day I'll take the res' of them, but I took a whole day off today so's jus' us three could go."

In the late afternoon they came back, a smiling trio, Martha's arms across the shoulders of her sons.

"We won't have so much fighting now," John said to Dave that night. "Martha took the boys to the woods today while I stayed at home and prayed. It cost us more money than we could well afford, but it was worth more than we dared risk. Martha's a wonderful mother. She had a long talk with each boy alone, then with the two together. She and the Lord are quite a team. Both those boys were saved today, and we had a jubilee time at supper tonight. We never can thank you enough, Dave, for opening our eyes."

Dave was sincerely glad for all of them. But for himself he had a sense of disappointment. He had started the work, but it took someone else to finish it. He had not known how.

Chapter 26

I wish I might have been with Martha and the boys on that picnic," said Dave to JoAnne several weeks later. "I would like to see how such a change could be accomplished. I made the diagnosis, but Martha wrought the cure."

"She doesn't think so," answered JoAnne slowly. "She talked to me about it out in the yard last night. She says she just took them to the Doctor who could and did cure them."

"Meaning?"

"You know what I mean, — or rather, Whom I mean? You could tell what was wrong, and Martha could talk all she pleased, and John could punish, but it took God to cure them. I don't know how it was done. Martha says He made them into 'new creatures in Christ.' "

Dave did not answer as he bent over the automobile he was making for Davie. JoAnne, as she ironed, prayed silently, "Lord, let him believe again as he used to. Let Him know that You are able to make us all new.

And let him believe that, *somehow* everything that happens to us is from Him."

The alarm clock on the table ticked noisily on. JoAnne finished the ironing and sat down to mend a pair of Davie's overalls. Dave, whistling softly, whittled on the wheels of the little car. Out in the alley the "gang" was breaking up for the night. Jud and Lute and Mary came up the walk laughing noisily. As they crossed the back porch Lute pulled a candy bar from his pocket and divided it with the other two.

"They do act like new creatures, don't they, Dave?"

"Yes, just at present. But the day isn't done yet."

"No — o," she said hesitantly. "But don't you think that the — the — grace that kept them through the day can still operate?"

"I suppose so, — or it can if they want it to badly enough."

"I'm sure they do. I believe they really mean it."

Dave whittled away until there was not enough of the small wheel to be worth anything. He threw it in the box of shavings and laid down his knife. When he spoke there was hesitation in his voice also.

"I guess you're right. There's another thing I'm thinking and wondering about. What happened to you, JoAnne? Did Martha work you over, too?"

JoAnne threaded her needle and carefully turned the edges of the patch before she spoke.

"Well, — it was partly Martha and partly Amy, but I suppose it was mostly God. It was too big a job for any human, or combination of humans, to do. I'm glad you've noticed it, Dave. That shows I'm making some

178

progress. What Martha did was to show me what I was. Then Amy came along and showed me the remedy. The old JoAnne was a vine that wrapped herself around other people until she almost choked them. The new JoAnne is trying to do her share of carrying the burdens of the world. Maybe that will help her to develop a stiffer backbone."

"You're all right, honey," came Dave's voice huskily. "You're the biggest little bit of all-right that I know of."

After another long silence he ventured, almost timorously, "What did you mean when you said 'the new JoAnne'? You said the boys were made 'new creatures in Christ' when they accepted Him. If you are new too, does it mean that you had never been a real Christian before?"

"Oh, no!" she cried. "I didn't mean that at all. I've been a Christian since I was eight. Nona was such an earnest Christian and she taught me so thoroughly that there was no chance for me not to understand. I believe I was really saved then. But I've been slow to grow. Amy showed me a chapter in Romans where Paul told of the struggle in him between the old and new man in Christ. That gave me a lot of help. If Paul had to fight, I shouldn't be ashamed that I had to. I'd like to tell you about it Dave, if you want to hear."

"Of course, I do!"

"It was one day last spring. Something had frightened me and I was all set for a spell of hysterics. You've seen them, Dave," she said, flushing, "and you know what I was like. Martha saw that it was no time for half-way measures. She did a most thorough job of snapping me out of it. She didn't really spank me, but she might as well have. I felt blistered all over. No — don't get angry or I won't tell you the rest. She didn't really hurt me, and I'm glad she did it. She showed me what a coward I had always been by letting everyone carry me all through life. I was — "

"You were all right. I never blamed you. I understood, and so did Nona, and we — "

"Yes, you did, bless your hearts! But you didn't help me to grow strong. Both of you spoiled me and shielded me and, — oh, Dave, I love you for it, but it wasn't what I needed. Even since you've been hurt you've been protecting me and I just stayed a 'fraid-cat.' But that day, Martha turned loose on me and oh, what a tongue-lashing she gave me! When she had reduced me to the right consistency or pliability or what-have-you, Amy Moxon took over and gave me some of the fundamentals of Christian living."

"Such as?"

"Faith — trust in God, — unselfishness, oh, a lot of them. I can't explain it all very well. I'm not very far advanced, and I'm not sure yet that I trust myself not to have a relapse in a tight place. But I'm learning. I have two good teachers. How such busy women find the time to study their Bibles so much, I don't know. They know just where to find what they need, and if I live to be eighty I may do them credit. At present, I feel very slow and stupid."

She stopped and looked earnestly at Dave, and her

face flushed as she went on into the more intimate part of her story.

"About being a new creation in Christ. I'll show you after while just where that is and you can read it for yourself. I've learned that in God's sight we really are new as soon as we're saved. Martha says that's because God looks at us through the blood of Christ and that covers everything under it. I found out, though, that even Paul didn't get rid of the old self entirely. It was always hanging around trying to defeat the new man."

"Just lies dormant much of the time, breaking out occasionally, as proved by Lute and Jud?"

"I guess it's different with each person. Some people seem not to have much trouble. With others it's a stiff battle. With me, the old JoAnne was just running everything. The new one didn't have a chance. Now, with Amy's and Martha's help, I'm trying to reverse their positions I hope I'm growing up, Dave. I really do want to be the kind of help to you that a woman should be."

Her voice was very humble as she spoke those last words, and Dave's eyes were misty as he put out one hand and drew her to his side.

"I loved the old JoAnne a lot, honey, but this new one is so dear to me that it chokes me up to try to tell her so."

Then he added the words that made her heart sing, "May I study with you? My new self needs to do a lot of growing up also."

So began for them a time of striving together to reach a place of peace. After years of suppression, it was not easy for the "new man" to gain the ascendency. The "old man" resisted the efforts to dethrone him. Amy was on hand often to help all that she could, and the young people drew strength and wisdom from her store. After each victory the going was easier and their confidence greater.

Dave had never overcome his unwillingness to see his former friends and, although they prayed about it, JoAnne and Amy did not speak of it any more. That was one of the things God would handle in His own time. Perhaps if Dad Brantwell had been there he could have helped. But it had been over two years since he had gone to New York on a business trip and become so ill that he had spent many months in the hospital there. During the first weeks after Dave's accident, Amy Moxon used to speak frequently of reports on his condition. All news from the store was carefully censored before it reached him, and no one was allowed to see him. When Amy realized that it pained Dave to hear any reference to his old friends, she ceased to speak of the old man. JoAnne often wondered about him. He had meant so much to her in the days of Nona's illness, and had been like a father on her wedding day. Had he retired to a life of invalidism? Had he forgotten the young man who had been his right hand for several years? Or did he leave them alone because Amy had told him of Dave's withdrawal from his old friends? Perhaps he was dead and Amy had not told them.

JoAnne, herself, often longed for a glimpse of the store and the friends with whom she had worked for years. But a passionate loyalty to Dave and his desires kept her away from them. Just now her entire life centered in the little apartment below the sidewalk, the three rooms that held Dave and Davie and all their love for each other. Some day when he was stronger Dave would be willing to open the doors to the world again. But for the present this little home was theirs alone. From it she went out every morning to earn their living, and to it she returned at night to find a glad welcome in the eyes of her boys.

Chapter 27

To Dave, in the absence of JoAnne, the days stretched out into unbelievably long hours, from eight o'clock in the morning when she gave Davie a last hug and put him down to turn and hold Dave close for a minute before a dash for the streetcar, to five-thirty when the watchers at the kitchen window would see her turn into the alley, arms full of groceries, and a smile on her face.

After that talk with JoAnne, Dave made an extra effort to fill in those long hours with something worthwhile. He gave Davie most careful care, he spent more time on the preparation of their meals, and he began a systematic review of his college textbooks. And one night he asked JoAnne what she thought of a correspondence course from the same school. She was delighted at the thought and when the lessons came she joined him in an interest in them.

Even with all this, however, the constant struggle against depression continued. Recently it had become so easy for him to lean on JoAnne that when she was away he felt restless and weak. The hours when she was at home became times of peace and relaxed nerves. As she grew stronger Dave had dropped his effort to spare her the sight of his moods. It was such a temptation to let go all the restraints and rest in her strength, that he did just that, and the former tenseness had disappeared. The evenings became carefree ones, — not with the lighthearted joyousness that had been theirs once, but with a freedom that comes when heavy burdens have been laid down for a time of rest.

During the days, however, in spite of all his attempts to overcome them the black moods would occasionally come. When John was at home his music was a strong tonic. Many a dark hour was brightened by music from harp or piano. Even the lessons of the beginners on violin or cornet were cheering to the listener. But there would come days when John had to be away, when the children whose noisy gaiety was diverting to him, were all in school and the two Daves were alone. Then it was that the silence became almost unendurable. Davie was a quiet baby, content to toddle about the three rooms or play quietly by Dave's chair. His vocabulary was limited to few words so there was little conversation. Even the books ceased to attract or interest. What did it profit to study when the knowledge gained could never be put to use?

On one of the darkest of these days he sat by the window watching the never ending procession of feet pass on the sidewalk. From Dave's viewpoint there were no bodies or heads. The high sidewalk brought the feet to the level of Dave's eyes, and the overhanging porch roof cut off all the legs below the knees. If only he could see *something* besides feet. What a relief it would be if someone went past, walking on his head, for a change! Then he fell to wondering what kind of heads belonged to those feet. That pair of worn work shoes must be matched by the huge body and head of a trucker from the warehouse down the street. Those runover oxfords would be worn by a heavy housewife out for her morn- ing shopping. The sloppy loafers that came next should be in school at this hour of the day.

So it went, all day long, — big feet, little feet, neat shoes, shabby shoes, new shoes and broken ones, — but all of them *walking*.

"Oh, God, why? Why? Why? Must I live out a long life tied to this chair and see JoAnne break under the burden of my care? My mind is as good as it ever was. I could do as good work as I ever did if I could get to the office. But here I am, good for nothing but to baby-sit and cook and play with jig-saw puzzles!"

At such times his thoughts turned often to the office at Brantwell's. Although he would not see any of his former associates he could not shut out the memory of them nor kill his interest in the work. What had become of Tony who first called JoAnne a "leeta, beeta keeda"? Did they ever clear up the dispute between Clark and McCoy? Did Slade run the whole store now or had Dad come back? He wished he had the courage to ask Amy Moxon about it. But although he knew he was growing less sensitive he could not yet talk about that life that had been so dear to him and was now gone forever. Perhaps someday he would be man enough to do it, but not now. That new self that JoAnne talked about was growing, but it was still quite a child.

Then he would remember Martha's admonition to her boys. "You got to feed your souls if you expec' 'em to grow. An' you can't do that readin' them so-called funnies. You got to feed 'em real food. Now you both read that chapter in the Bible, an' when I get this washin' done we'll all discuss it 'fore we go to bed."

So Dave would get his own Bible, and in its pages find the strength and assurance he needed. Then while Davie took his nap he prayed, — prayed for JoAnne that God would bless and keep her and enable her to be happy in spite of the heavy burdens she bore. He prayed for Davie that he might grow up strong and good, able to do a man's work in the world and never know the agonies of frustration. He prayed with thanksgiving for Amy and Martha and John. Then he asked for himself that he might feel life surging through his dead limbs again, and so be able, even though handicapped, to care for his dear ones.

Gradually his prayers for himself changed. At first he prayed for physical healing with an intensity which brooked no denial. For had he not read the story of the importunate widow whose prayer was answered because she was determined it should be? But as he read more and more from the Book he began to get a longer view, — the will of God for human lives. The insistence left his praying and in its stead came humility. He still prayed for healing, but now it was "if it be Thy will."

He became interested in the Book of Romans. The seventh chapter showing Paul's struggle with his old nature was very real to him. Did he not have the same

struggles himself? Then how wonderful was the assurance of the eighth chapter, climaxing in those last words!

> Who shall separate us from the love of Christ?
> Shall tribulation or distress or persecution,
> Or famine, or nakedness, or peril, or sword?
> As it is written, For thy sake we are killed
> All the day long; we are accounted
> As sheep for the slaughter.
> Nay, in all these things we are more than conquerors
> Through him who loved us.
> For I am persuaded that neither death nor life nor angels,
> Nor principalities nor powers,
> Nor things present, nor things to come,
> Nor height, nor depth, nor any other creature
> Shall be able to separate us from the love of God
> Which is in Christ Jesus our Lord.

Then he read on until he reached the twelfth chapter.
Here he got no farther than the second verse. His whole
being was awed by the realization of what it might
mean.

"Your bodies a living sacrifice! The good and acceptable and perfect will of God!"

Over and over he pondered it, and when John came
in to prepare him for bed he questioned,

"Jawn, do you know Romans twelve?"

"I certainly do! Not that I can repeat it all. I'm
not as good as Martha at memorizing. But I *know* it,
— it's all in me, I mean. It's wonderful!"

"What do you think it means? What does it say to
you, those first two verses?"

John paused in his rubbing as if this were too important a subject to be shared with anything else.

"What does it mean? Well, Dave, when I first met those verses face to face I was in the middle of the toughest time I ever had. I had applied for a job that I knew I was very well qualified to fill. And I needed that job desperately. I was turned down because of my color and I was pretty bitter. Then one night I heard a sermon on those verses and they just broke me all up. That night I gave my whole body to God, black skin and all, to fulfill as far as possible His perfect will. Because Christ died for me that sacrifice was holy and acceptable to Him, and I've never tried to take it back. I'm not very fine to look at, and I'll never make a big mark in the world. But all that I am and have belong to Him. Glory hallelujah!"

Dave reached for JoAnne's hand as she stood there beside him and held it tightly as he said in a voice that was shaking but somehow had in it a note of victory,

"That's what I want to do, too. My body isn't worth much, but I want Him to take it and do with it just what He wills!"

Stooping over him to kiss him she answered earnestly, "Me too, Dave."

Chapter 28

FROM THE DAY that Dave gave up the fight and let himself rest in the will of the Lord who had been a sacrifice for him, life took on more meaning for both him and JoAnne. Since the night he had cried in JoAnne's arms he had been striving to achieve peace and a belief in God's love for him. He had fought doubt and despair and had tried desperately to find the well in his valley of Baca. Now he struggled no more. He had presented his body to the perfect will of God. The years would reveal what that will was.

Amy Moxon, meeting the minister who had tried to help them many months before, told him the story.

"It's the greatest spiritual victory that I ever witnessed. You can call on him now, pastor. I know he will be glad to see you. You will probably be helped yourself, as I have been."

The minister did call and spent an hour in the room where he had expected to spend fifteen minutes. They talked of the lessons Dave was studying and went on from there to discuss the Bible course he was taking.

Their spirits drew together over the Word and they spoke of the deep and precious things of God. When the minister left he carried with him a blessing that overflowed on every home or hospital bed he visited for many a day.

Martha and John talked about it as they sat together one night after the children were in bed.

"He's a sure nuff changed boy, Jawn. It's like a miracle."

John agreed. "He wasn't ever ugly or mean. He was always gentle and kind. But he was moody and low in spirit. Many a time I've rubbed him for half an hour and never a word would he say. I've often wondered what kind of a chap he was before he was hurt."

"He's been lots better ever since that time JoAnne heard him hystericin' an' I had to give her a dressin' down. She did somethin' for him that day."

"You did something for her first, Martha, and she just passed it on. They've both been changing all summer and fall, but all of a sudden in that twelfth chapter of Romans Dave quit trying an' let loose in God's hands. You know that little prayer we sing at church, 'Break me, melt me, mold me, fill me.' Well, that's all happened to Dave."

"Yes, an' now he's got a glory, an' it's spillin' on ever'body he meets."

To JoAnne the days in the office were uninteresting stretches of time that had to be lived through before she could go home to the joy that waited her. Dave would have supper ready, and after it was eaten and the dishes washed there would be an hour of play with Davie, then together they would put him to bed. In the front room they would read or study or play games. Or more often they would just sit and talk, recounting the day's events and laughing over the haps and mishaps that came their way. Each talk finally turned to spiritual things, for Dave could not keep his new-found joy out of his conversation. They would have devotions together before John came to put him to bed. Then after John had gone and she came to tell him good night he would smile in contentment and say,

"We have good times together, don't we, keeda? The well in our valley has turned into a fountain, JoAnne."

One of the happiest phases of it all to JoAnne was that Dave took his old place of leadership in their lives. Once more she found herself leaning on his strength.

"I'm glad it happened before I made a bad mistake," she thought one night just before sleep came. "I'm not as brave as they think I am, and I've felt sometimes as if I couldn't take life any longer. But I knew that if I went to pieces it would be bad for Dave. I can't tell anyone else how afraid I've been but, God, I do thank You for making Dave able to help again. Even with a fountain in the valley I can do with a lot of help."

On an afternoon in January when snow-filled gray clouds made the room dark in midafternoon, Dave laid aside his books and sat alone in the dusk. Davie was asleep in the bedroom and the apartment was quiet except for the sound of the music lessons next door. A young church pianist was practicing hymns and Dave sang softly to her accompaniment.

Peace, peace, wonderful peace!
Coming down from the Father above.
Sweep over my spirit forever, I pray
In fathomless billows of love.

A sound at the door startled him, and he turned to stare in amazement at the two men who stood there. Then with a glad cry of "Dad!" he reached out his hands. The old man broke away from the chauffeur who was holding his arm, to stoop over the chair and hold Dave close as he said in a broken voice,

"Oh, my boy, my boy! What have they done to you! And why didn't I know this?"

"It's — it's g-good to see you. I've wanted you — so many times. But — but please don't feel badly, sir. I'm happier now than I ever was in my whole life. All I needed was to see you again."

The chauffeur drew up a chair that Mr. Brantwell might sit close by, and then the years were reviewed. Again and again the old man would reach for Dave's hand and grip it tightly as he sensed some of the struggle the young man had passed through.

"And what about that doll of a wife of yours? Have you been able to reassure her during this hard time? Has she accepted it as happily as you have?"

Dave laughed. "My doll of a wife has grown into a woman, Dad, the finest woman in the world. She has done the reassuring for me. And she's a grand little mother. Oh, didn't Amy tell you about our boy? He will wake up soon. You're going to stay for dinner with us and see both of them."

"Really, I shouldn't."

"But you *should*. Let Harry take the car home and come back for you at nine. Please do, sir. We've wanted you for so long!"

He could not refuse even had he desired, and he admitted to himself that he did not desire. So when JoAnne came it was to find Dave at work in the kitchen while Davie sat contentedly on Mr. Brantwell's knees. She greeted him joyfully and the old man watched her as she turned to help Dave with the meal. Almost every trace of the timid girl had disappeared. The thick glasses were still worn, but the hesitating diffidence had been replaced by a confident poise that gave assurance of mature womanhood. The evening he spent with them warmed his heart, from the simple dinner for which they offered no apologies, to the picture he carried away with him of JoAnne with Davie in her arms standing by Dave's chair and all of them radiating their joy at his return to them.

The news of Dave's injury had been a terrible shock to him on his recent return to the store after his long absence. He had longed to see him, yet dreaded to come. Now, as he left, he knew he had been blessed and would be returning again and again to the little home below the sidewalk.

Dr. Herman, when he heard from Amy Moxon of Dave's changed state of mind, grunted a bit skeptically.

"I wish I could believe it to be genuine and permanent. He puts on that act for JoAnne's sake, and the effort he makes tenses his nerves almost to breaking. Then he has a blow-up again and we're back right where we started."

"This will be permanent."

"I'm not so sure. He's a good actor."

"He's not acting now. He's genuinely happy, not syn-thetically so as he has been these past months when he put on a brave front."

"I'd like to believe that but I'll have to see it."

"Go and see him then," she said quietly. "You'll see something that will open your eyes."

Go he did and came away to believe.

"He's happy," he admitted. "And what is more im-portant, he is utterly relaxed. If there's the slightest pos-sibility that those seemingly dead muscles will ever show life, this thing that has happened, no matter what you call it, should help. But I didn't tell him that, and don't you mention it. There's just one chance in a thousand and I don't want their hopes stirred up."

He watched Dave more closely for several weeks, but saw no signs of improvement and at last he said to Mr. Brantwell,

"I'm ready to quit. As far as I can tell, from every test I know how to make, there isn't a thing wrong with his legs. But in spite of that he can't move, and I don't think he ever will."

Mr. Brantwell sighed in disappointment. "There goes my dream. I've been hoping that he could have artificial feet fitted and be back in the store before long."

"That's what we planned at first. The best men at the hospital were sure it would be only a matter of a few months. But it's over two years. I'm sure now that he will never be better. He will be tied to that chair for life."

"Well, if he can't go to the store I'll take the store to him. I don't know how I'll manage it, but I will. I need that boy."

Resolutely he began to carry out his intention. He had a telephone installed in Dave's room. Every morning there were long conferences over the personnel problems and plans. Then a messenger would be dispatched to carry a briefcase full of papers out for Dave's perusal. He would study them, make notes, and have them all ready for the chauffeur to pick up before he went to the office for Mr. Brantwell. After a few weeks of this work a typewriter was sent out, and soon the clatter of its keys drowned out the noise of John's music.

"Oh, it's good to be at work again!" Dave cried, as JoAnne entered one evening to find him gathering up his papers. "And listen, Mrs. Robertson, we're going to have to go back to the schedule we kept in the old days when we were young. I've been so busy I forgot to get supper!"

JoAnne laughed as she looked at the stove where no steaming kettle awaited. "That will be fun. Do you remember how I used to rush out and start the potatoes before I took my coat off? It was fun then and it's fun now. We'll get supper together."

As if the years had dropped away they worked, Dave rolling his chair from cabinet to table while JoAnne attended to the things on the stove, and Davie from his high chair laughed, thinking it a game. When they sat at the table and Dave bowed his head to send up to God a prayer of thanksgiving for the food and all the other blessings in their lives, JoAnne felt as if she could not contain such happiness. The well in their valley had overflowed and watered the desert and all sorts of flowers were blooming there.

Chapter 29

IT HAD BEEN a rather trying morning. Each day the volume of work from the store had increased and the hours were full. As Dave read or typed he kept an eye on Davie who had reached the climbing age.

"If you don't behave yourself, Pudge, I'll have to put you in your pen," he cautioned, pulling the youngster down from a precarious perch on a chair arm. "Here, take your hammer and pound those pegs in the board."

Davie pounded for a few minutes, then wandered off again. Dave, intent on his work, did not miss him until the sound of splashing water made him hurry to the kitchen as fast as he could propel his chair. Davie was in the sink, and so thoroughly soaked that he required a complete change of clothing.

"Listen, fella, have a heart!" said Dave pleadingly. "I don't think it's quite cricket for you to move so fast. Your old man is handicapped and can't keep up. Can't you behave for just a little while? Then Mommy will be home and you can belong to her for the rest of the day."

"Thwat?"

"I said can't you be *good*?"

"Dood. Davie dood."

"You are *not!* But — oh, I love you anyway!"

He pulled the clean overalls on over the sturdy little legs and breathed a prayer.

"God, keep him well and strong, and guard these little feet from accident!"

From one thing to another the baby trotted. Dave tried again and again to interest him in some "sedentary job" but Davie preferred activity.

"I can see now that if I expect to be worth a paycheck to Brantwell's I'll have to hire me a baby-sitter," Dave said as he pulled the little hands out of a dresser drawer. "Or maybe — I hardly dare dream it — I can get to the place where JoAnne can stay home with us. If only — Pudge, get off that table! I sure hope you take a long nap this afternoon. I think I'll get Doc to give you a seda-tive!"

After a few more escapades Dave gave up his effort to work. "Perhaps we'd better eat some lunch. Maybe that will make you sleepy. Come on, let's heat the soup Mommy left for us."

Back in the kitchen, with the soup boiling on the stove, Dave turned to the cabinet for their dishes. Stuck to the door was a note from JoAnne. She often left one in some odd place to remind him of some duty or tell him a bit of news.

> Just to remind you, when this note shall find you,
> That if you have time today,
> You might put a shine on those brown shoes of mine.
> Just now they are grubby and gray.

Chuckling at this "punch-up" on a promise he had made her several days ago, he deftly turned his chair. Then, as he faced the stove again he sat transfixed with panicky fear. Davie had pulled his highchair close to the stove and had climbed into it. Standing up, he was leaning toward the stove trying to reach the red and white salt shaker on top of the oven. One inch farther would mean a tumble, and if he fell the boiling soup would go with him. There was no time to waste. Dave did not stop to think. He acted.

John, preparing lunch for his children in his own kitchen heard the crash and came running. Dave and Davie were on the floor together, Davie screaming with fright and Dave staring wildly.

"What happened, Dave? What happened?" he asked, ignoring the crying child. "How did you fall?"

He stooped and gathered Dave into his arms. He carried him to the bed and ran his hands over the back and limbs to discover if there might be any injuries.

"How did it happen?" he persisted. "How did you happen to fall?"

Dave's teeth chattered in nervous shock. "Get Davie, Jawn, and tie him to my bed. I have to see him. Thanks. I'll be better soon. I'm not hurt, really I'm not. I'm just shaken — you see I didn't fall, Jawn — I jumped!"

In spite of John's incredulity he persisted in that assertion. John called Dr. Herman who came out at once and gave Dave a complete and thorough examination. He found nothing to indicate any change in the condition that had existed for two and a half years.

"The boy fell," he told Amy Moxon. "I don't know

how he did it,— leaned over too far and the chair slipped, or something like that. It's a wonder he wasn't injured."

But Dave was not disturbed by the skepticism of the doctor. "I know what happened," he said calmly. "I did *not* fall. I jumped. I can't do it now, and I probably never will again. But I jumped then. When I saw Davie reach across that kettle and knew that if I yelled he'd fall, I jumped and grabbed him. I *know!*"

He did not want it told to JoAnne. "She might think it means something and then she'd be disappointed again. We are happy so we won't disturb her about it. It will probably never occur again."

The doctor came more frequently for awhile, and John labored more diligently at the morning and evening massagings, but the limbs lay as unresponsive as ever. The others were all sure that in some inexplicable way Dave had fallen, and he did not argue with them.

Chapter 30

As WINTER BEGAN to blow its way out, and signs of spring came even to the shabby triangle that lay between the busy street and two railroad tracks, dreams of the little home they had planned in the country came to taunt JoAnne. Davie was old enough now to want to get out of doors when he saw the other children playing. How would they ever dare let him out with no one to watch him? Yet he could not stay in the house all the time. Also, it was becoming evident that if Dave were to do any work at home he could not be hampered by having to take care of a lively two-year-old boy. For the best good of them all it was important that Dave be helped in every way possible to rehabilitate himself. Perhaps sometime he could be able to earn enough that they could hire someone to care for Davie and do the housework. But what to do *now*? The only answer was a day nursery, but as the thought came to her she felt a wave of terror sweep over her. She could not understand it, for why should the thought of a day nursery be a terrifying one? Then a picture came to her mind,— a picture that seemed to have some fearful meaning to her.

Was it from some story one of the girls at the Home had told her? Or had she read it long ago? It was a picture of a roomful of children — one shy little tot that stumbled and fell and bumped into things — a hard hand that clutched her arm and dragged her away — an even darker room — a closed door — utter panic. JoAnne did not know where that picture fitted into her life, but it was only when she had turned from the window where she had been standing, to the lighted room behind her, that she was able to banish the cold fear that held her. Of one thing she was sure. Davie should never go to a day nursery, unless it be in some church or neighborhood house where she knew the ones who would care for him. At present she knew of no such place, but she would seek one. She was determined that Dave should have his chance and that Davie should not grow up under the shadow of fear.

She came out of the office of the box factory one afternoon in April to find Mr. Brantwell waiting in his car.

"I want to talk to you alone, JoAnne," he said. "Let's take a little ride before you go home. We won't stay long, so Dave won't have time to worry. Go out to the Park and drive around it, Harry."

As they drove he told her of plans he had made which waited only for Dave's and her approval before being put into execution.

"Don't you think Dave is better for having some work to do?"

"Oh, yes, much! At least he's *happier*. I don't know about his health but Dr. Herman says he's fine. He certainly loves to be at work again. The other night when you sent out those papers marked 'Urgent — please rush!' he paid a little neighbor girl to help me with the dishes in his place, and if a wheel chair can strut, his did!"

Mr. Brantwell laughed. "Well, let him be as cocky as he wants to. Down at the office everyone is pleased beyond expression to be in touch with him again. And just to know that he is here for me to call on in an emergency is a tremendous help to me in these days when I'm only about half a man myself."

JoAnne said nothing, knowing that he would go on when he was ready.

"But that's not enough," he continued. "I need Dave back in the office where I can get him at once when I need him. And there are cases every day where I want him to talk to the persons involved. He needs to be there in the thick of things for his own good, also. Dr. Herman says he is thoroughly well except for those useless limbs, but that he needs some outdoor air and sunshine. John has done an excellent job. I'm glad you have lived where he could help Dave.

"Here's what I want to do. I want to send him to a hospital in Arizona where they train people in his condition to make the best use of what's left to them. There are certain exercises he can take which will strengthen and harden him. While he is down there I want to get artificial feet for him."

"But he can't *use* them!"

"I know it. But he can look at them and so can the world. I know it would contribute a lot to my morale to have a pair of feet at the end of my long legs! I believe that, in that case, he might be willing to lay aside that blanket he now hangs onto so grimly. It will make him feel more like the rest of us again. At least, that's my logic, and Dr. Herman says it can't hurt anything."

"Is Dave willing to go? Have you seen him?"

"No-o. That's why I wanted to see you first. You see it may take six months to get him into condition again, and you'd have to carry on alone here while he's away."

"I could do that if it would help him to get back to the office. But *how* would it help? How could we get him to the office even if he were strong? He can't do anything without his chair."

"We'll manage that all right. We'll get both him and the chair there, or we'll have a chair at each end of the line. That can all be fixed up when we get the boy taken care of. He can't run all over the store as he did before, but folks can come to him."

JoAnne's eyes misted at the thought of what all of this would mean to Dave if it could be done. But she thought of Dave's independent spirit, and asked anxiously,

"Could he really be worth much to you?"

"As much as ever. In fact, more. For now, added to his natural instinct for understanding human nature, there is a sympathy for the unfortunate that he did not have before. Yes, indeed he will be valuable. My board members are all back of me in this. They all want him."

"But we can't afford it, and you know Dave won't let you pay for six months in a hospital!"

"He won't have to. There was no sense in Slade letting this thing drag on for so long. The insurance company, the contractor, and our lawyer had a conference yesterday, and there will be plenty of money for all expenses. You may wish to keep on working while he is away, but if Dave does as well as the doctor expects, you will be able to quit working when he gets back."

"Oh, that would make Dave happier than anything else. But Davie will be a problem with Dave gone."

"You're a practical lady for such a small one. Amy Moxon thought of a solution to that. If we send out work from the store you could type at home, couldn't you?"

"Yes. But don't just *make* a job for me."

"You independent children! No, I assure you it's a real job and you'll work as hard as you do now. Does that satisfy you?"

Dave, when he heard all the details of the plan was unexpectedly docile and willing. The hope that he could again support his family, and the knowledge that it was money from the insurance company that would pay the bill, were all that were needed to convince him.

On the last afternoon before he left he and JoAnne sat together by the window, not saying much but feeling deeply the fact that, for the first time since they were married, they were to be separated.

"I hope there will be some lovely sunrises where you are going," she said softly. "I hope you have an east window where you can see it across the full stretch of the horizon."

"When I see the sunrise there I'll think that just two hours before it was sunrise back home where my heart is. I love sunrises, but for the next six months they are going to be especially welcome because each one means that one more day has come, and I'm that much nearer home."

"I can't see a sunrise from here, but I'll know when a new day comes anyway, and I'll pray, 'Dear God, please help Dave today. Keep him close to Thee, and bring him back to Davie and me.' Then I'll go and make another check on my calendar."

"And all day long I'll be praying for you. If I have to lie and soak up Arizona sunshine I'll have lots of time to pray. Oh, JoAnne, do you know how precious you are to me? You will never know how wonderful you have seemed to me this last year. I've just felt like I'd let go and was resting on your love."

"Thank you for saying that. I've tried *so* hard to grow up and be a real wife. At times I haven't felt like I was succeeding. But if it meant that to you I must have done better than I thought."

"Only God knows how well you did do. I didn't believe last year that I ever would enjoy life again. I thought I had to keep up so that you'd be able to carry on, and give Davie half a chance. For myself, I didn't expect anything. I didn't let you know it, but there were times when I thought I'd go crazy. I didn't care for a God who would let a life be smashed as mine had been. All that kept me going at all was your need of me. I couldn't go and leave you alone to face a world you'd always been afraid of.

"Then one night when things were blackest,— when I knew I couldn't go on without cracking up — you remember that night, don't you, darling?" His voice broke and his arm tightened around her shoulders. "I had reached the lowest spot I'd ever been in. I was sure I couldn't go on another day. Then you came and put your arms around me and I forgot that you were the one I was supposed to hold up. You seemed like my mother that night. And I let go just like I used to in her arms. You told me how God could make a well in our valley of bitterness, and then you sang. I think it was that little off-key lullaby that finished me. I'd heard you sing it to Davie dozens of times, and it was just the thing I needed. I felt so weak and — and — young and — as if I had no strength or will of my own. So I let loose of all the pride and determination that had been keeping me going, and I relaxed on your strength. Oh, honey, it was such blessed rest."

After a time of silence that was as satisfying as speech he began again. "Then you went on showing me day after day that the well was there, and even when I didn't feel like making the effort for myself, you held the cup to my lips and I was refreshed. I knew that you had no real strength of your own so I began to read my Bible to find out what was helping you. Then I found that twelfth chapter of Romans and it — well, it just *got* me. Until then I'd been stumbling along, rising, falling, one day up, the next down, never quite forgetting my useless body and secretly rebelling against it, and living on your strength. If you had failed I'd have gone down. But that day I gave Christ my body and it's been His ever since. If He wants me to glorify Him from a wheel chair all my life, that's exactly what I want to do. From now on I am Christ's and He is God's."

They sat quietly, she on one of Davie's small chairs at his side, her head leaning against his arm. Through the window they could see the embankment which led to the sidewalk and street. When they came here it had been bare and ugly but now it was covered with vines that were just beginning to show their first delicate green. Above the street they could see the irregular line of rooftops and factory chimneys which, all day long, were shrouded in a blanket of smoke.

"It isn't a very pretty view, is it?" asked Dave. "There have been days when I felt as ugly and cheerless as that. But now that I'm leaving, it's suddenly rather dear to me. We've been pretty happy here this last year, haven't we?"

"Yes, and we — oh, look Dave! Can you see? Lean over this way a little more. There — between those two buildings!"

The breeze had blown the smoke away, and in the space where a low building squatted between two tall ones, a glorious sunset shone. It was only a tiny spot between the ugly chimneys, the black funnels, and the unsightly buildings. But in that small compass shone a riot of color, changing ever from one iridescent pattern to another. They watched it until it faded and the gray smoke closed in again.

"What a good-by!" said Dave. "I'm going to take it for a promise too,— a promise of a tomorrow when I can come home and do a real man's work again."

But after he had fallen asleep, JoAnne lay on her bed crying into her pillow. "I'm not at all brave like they think I am. I feel like screaming this minute. I don't want him to go, and I'm afraid to stay here without him. But this time I won't scream if it kills me. I won't!"

Chapter 31

THE DAYS AFTER DAVE was taken away resolved themselves into a succession of monotonously regular hours strung on the thread of time, and each having to be lived through before Dave could come home. The one redeeming feature of those hours was that, as they passed, they could not help but bring him closer. Each evening JoAnne crossed off another day from the calendar, and once a week she counted the remaining ones as they stretched ahead to the end of the six months Mr. Brantwell had mentioned. The living room where for over two years Dave had lived and fought and won, seemed too empty. JoAnne rearranged the few pieces of furniture, but the result did not lift her spirits. Dave was still gone, and the little apartment echoed with emptiness.

She kept busy looking after Davie, cooking, cleaning, doing the laundry, and typing all afternoon and evening on the work sent out from the office. She was determined to earn the salary she was paid, and she knew from experience what a day's output should be. So she worked long after Davie was asleep, and asked for more and more work until she was satisfied that the dollars in her pay envelope were rightfully hers. Amy Moxon kept an eye on her lest she overdo, but decided after a few weeks that the work was a blessing in that it sent her to bed weary every night.

What Amy did not know was that the night hours were not all spent in sleeping. More often than not JoAnne would hear the streamliner whistle for the crossing at two o'clock before she slept. She was ashamed to tell this to Amy, for she knew that the nurse thought she had conquered her cowardice. Martha seemed to sense the situation, for without saying anything she left the studio door ajar at night. Observing this, JoAnne opened her own door. It helped greatly to know that across the hall John and Martha were within hearing distance. For at night, with the work of the day over, with Davie's chatter stilled, with no children whooping in the back yard, and only the stealthy, unrecognizable night sounds to be heard, she had to admit to herself that she was not only lonesome and heartsick for Dave, but she was frightened. Frightened with all the old panic and terror that had been a part of her childhood.

"I'm just as big a coward as I ever was," she moaned one night. "After all that big talk I gave Dave to cheer him up, I can't do a thing with myself. The old bogeyman is still after me. The only thing I've gained is the ability to hide it. I don't scream anymore. I just feel like it and frizzle all up inside of me and hurry off to crawl under somebody's wing and hide my head. And this time I have to fight it out alone. I can't run to Amy or Mr. Brantwell or they might tell Dave. And he mustn't know. But I'm scared. I'm just plain scared! Don't like to live alone, and I hate the dark. I'm afraid when the wind blows and I'm afraid when it rains. What's the matter with me, anyway?"

Night after night she argued with herself, trying to banish the impulse to hysteria which beset her. She feared the sounds outside her window, the shadows that hung close to the building and lay below the sidewalk. She put Davie's crib close beside her each night so that she could touch him without getting out of bed. The feeling of his warm little body always brought reassurance, and she often fell asleep with her hand over his fist.

"What a great big 'fraid-cat I am!" she whispered. "I'm even running to my baby for protection."

Resolutely she kept her fears hidden, however, and her letters to Dave gave no hint of them. She wrote a letter every evening as soon as Davie had been put to bed. Each morning's mail brought one from Dave. That link with him was her greatest morale builder, and the knowledge of his trust in her carried her through many hard days.

His letters were like Dave, breezy, cheerful, and full of love and concern for his dear ones. The trip to the sanitarium had been a thrilling experience to one who had spent two years in a small apartment where even a glimpse of the horizon was denied him. He wrote at length about the details of those two days on the train. But it had been a tiring ordeal and several weeks had to be spent in bed before any regular treatments or exercises could begin. There was a bright spot in those days in bed, however,— a happening that made Dave so happy that his letter telling about it brought tears to JoAnne's eyes as she comprehended how much it meant to him.

213

The letter came a week before his birthday. "Do you know what the twentieth is, Mrs. Robertson? It's your husband's birthday. And I want to order my gift. You were going to give me one, weren't you? Well, I want a dozen pairs of socks,— the loudest, flashiest socks Brantwell's have. And if you want to put in a couple of ties to match, that will be all right with me, too. You see, honey, I have a brand new pair of feet! I can't walk on them but they are here anyway, and when I can get out of bed I'll dress them up in some socks and shoes and just sit and look at them. I had them on for awhile today and in spite of their size, which is the same old number ten, they are handsome! You might send those socks that are in the bottom drawer of the chiffonier. You've been thinking I didn't know you were saving them, haven't you? Well, I knew, though I could never figure why. Send them along. I don't know how I can wear holes in socks when my feet won't move. But I'll manage. I have a mighty yearning to see you darning my socks again. I'll do it if I have to use a file on them!"

At first he wrote fully and enthusiastically about his exercises and massages. He even told casually about the shock treatments that were painful to the rest of his body but did not affect the legs at all. He described, in detail worthy of a new and long desired automobile, the wheel chair he was to use.

"I don't know how Dad expects to manage it, but he promises that he will have me down at the office before Christmas. I really am much stronger. I sit up all day, and I'm pitcher on our ball team. Can you get a picture of us chasing around the diamond in our chairs? Compared to even sandlot games it's pretty slow, I guess. But to us it's a difficult and dangerous pastime. Donkey baseball isn't in it for real thrills."

JoAnne rejoiced in his enthusiasm, was happy in his progress, and dreamed of the time when he would be back with her. Mr. Brantwell had regular reports from the superintendent, and often he would bring them out for her to read.

"He'll be back here before we know it," he said. "I'm going to have my old pick-up truck fitted out so that his chair can be rolled right up into it. Then we'll take Dave and the chair up in the freight elevator when we get to the store. The day that boy gets back in my office I'll begin to function again as an executive."

JoAnne's heart grew lighter and she began once more to plan for the future. With Dave going to work each morning, even though it be in a wheel chair, and coming home to her each night, life would again fall into a normal pattern. They might even get a house of their own. It could not be in the country of course, for Harry would have to come for Dave in the truck, but it could have a back yard where Davie could play and where she could grow some flowers. With such an alluring prospect before her she surely could control her fears a few months longer.

In August a letter came that seemed to mark the apex of his pleasure in his new freedom.

"I caught a guy out, JoAnne; I caught him out slick as a whistle. I've done it many a time before, but never from a chair! It has been the sensation of the 'campus' ever since. All that noise you heard from off in the west

215

was *not* thunder. It was cheering for Big Boy Robertson, the first fellow on our team to show that he was big league stuff."

Not long after that JoAnne began to notice a difference in his letters. He wrote as often as before, but the letters said less about himself, and were, instead, filled with the sayings and doings of his mates. Mr. Brantwell was away, so that his reports also were missing. Amy Moxon was on vacation and Dr. Herman was busy with the polio cases that were assuming almost epidemic proportions. There was no one else whom she could ask, so her only source of information was the letters which told her nothing as to Dave's condition. She opened each one eagerly, hoping it would contain some news as to progress and expectations. But day after day there was news of others, of Bill who went home to open a little store; of Henry who would not co-operate with the doctors; of Pat, whom they called Melchior because of his tenor voice. There was frequent reference to the pastor of the near-by church who came out and held Bible classes twice a week and occasionally played checkers and chess with them. But nothing of Dave.

When Mr. Brantwell came back in early September, she called him. Yes, he had had a report last week and all was well. He would let her know if he got any different news. His voice sounded abstracted and JoAnne was smitten with compunction for taking the time of such a busy man merely to bolster up her weakening morale. Surely she, who heard from Dave himself every day, should not bother others. Amy Moxon was getting a new hospital insurance plan instituted in the store and her calls on the telephone or in person were hurried and rare. Martha and John were busy "from kin see to cain't see" as Martha put it, and except for the sound of music lessons which told of John's presence in the house, JoAnne might have lived alone. The Katz and Polowsky children, as well as Martha's brood, were all at school. Miss Melton was at work, and her songs were not there to break the silence. Life seemed to have reached a stale mate, each day exactly like the others and none bringing promise of a change.

Chapter 32

F ALL DAYS CAME ON, rather more dark and gloomy than usual. October, which normally was a time of colored leaves, bright skies and tangy breezes, was cold and rainy. It was easy for JoAnne's thoughts to take color from the weather. She was sure that Dave was not doing well and that they were keeping the real facts from her. She began again to wonder about the future and fear clutched her heart. Why, oh why, had she consented to Dave being taken away? What if this venture should prove to be too much for him? Perhaps he had injured himself in some way, maybe by that wonderful catch in the ball game that had so thrilled him. Perhaps he would have to be brought home to live in a cast,— or maybe not brought home at all! What would she do if she had to learn to face life for herself and Davie with no beloved invalid in his wheel chair by the window? Could she bear to come back after a day's work and know that he would never be there to greet her again?

It was all very well to talk of being brave, to hunt for

springs in your valley or, finding no springs, to dig there a well. But that was for strong people, for those who knew how to walk alone or who could be cheerful when their hearts were like lead, for those who had never known the cold clutch of fear. It was not for her. All her life she had fought her weakness and tried to be brave and strong, and it was no use. She was weak and had to have someone to lean on. Surely God knew how much she needed Dave. He *couldn't* be taken from her. She *had* to have him, even if he never got out of their little home again. With him there she could face what life would bring even if all her other plans and dreams had to go. But she had to have Dave. He was her strength.

During one gloomy week when the rain fell from the eaves in a monotonous drizzle and dirty water ran down the window panes and backed up under the sills, she became more despondent than usual.

"It's this house," she decided. "It gives me the *spookiest* feeling. It reminds me of something but I don't know what. It's like a dream that I've had, but all the details are gone when I wake up, and only a sense of — of — something weird remains. I keep feeling as if something might grab me."

That feeling increased as the days passed, until she began to fear the coming of nightfall. If Amy had not been so busy she would have asked the kind nurse to spend a few nights with her. She considered calling the Home where she had been raised, and asking if one of the older girls might come in each night. But she did not know the present matron and could expect no such sympathetic understanding of her problem as Mrs. Sperry would have given.

"I don't really think anything will harm us," she reasoned. "In fact, I'm *sure* we'll be O.K. But what my brain believes and what my backbone feels are two different things! There's something about this house that makes my spinal column turn to water."

As night drew on, after a day that had been discouraging from the receipt of Dave's noncommittal letter in the morning to the breaking of her typewriter in the late afternoon, JoAnne sank wearily into the chair by the kitchen table. She was chilly and tired. The furnace had not been drawing well, and its half-hearted efforts to heat the house had been completely defeated by the wind and rain. Davie had kept her awake for two nights with a deep bronchial cough, and she did not see how she could endure another such session as last night had been. Just now he was sleeping but his restlessness presaged another hard night in spite of the doctor's medicines.

Almost too weary to care what she did, she reached out her hand to the Bible that lay on the table. It was the one they had used for morning readings during those last weeks before Dave left, the one he had studied so eagerly and from which he had drawn strength and comfort. He had left it with her and carried with him the new one that Amy had given him for a farewell gift. All through this one were markings that told her of passages that were especially dear to him. Turning page after page she read them, feeling drawn closer to him as she did it. Then, back in a part of the Old Testament where it had eluded her for all the weeks, was a sheet of paper with references on it, written in Dave's scrawl-ing handwriting. It was headed, HIS PRESENCE, and a number of references followed. With the sensation of walking over ground that he had trodden before her, she read them, and as she read she felt almost stunned by knowledge that came to her, the knowledge that Dave was not always brave and strong, that even after his surrender of his entire being to God he still had to seek strength from the Source of all strength.

She followed the list of references reading each one with a growing appreciation of the reality of such promises:

> Be strong and of a good courage, fear not, nor be afraid of them; for the Lord thy God, he it is that doth go with thee; he will not fail thee nor forsake thee.
> And the Lord, he it is that doth go before thee; he will be with thee; he will not fail thee, neither forsake thee: fear not, neither be dismayed.
> In thy presence is fullness of joy.
> My presence shall go with thee and I will give thee rest.
> God is our refuge and our strength, a very *present* help in trouble.
> Fear thou not for I am with thee . . . . I the Lord will hold thy right hand saying unto thee, Fear not.
> When thou passest through the waters I will be with thee.
> I will never leave thee nor forsake thee.
> Lo, I am with you *alway*, even unto the end of the world.

That "alway" was underlined, and something was writ-ten at the side along the margin. Turning the book she read through tear-dimmed eyes.

"Yes, *always,* so we are never alone, therefore cannot

fear. Always with JoAnne and me whether we are apart or together. Thank You, Lord."

Suddenly the wonder of it swept over her like a flood. Jesus Christ, her Saviour and Lord, God's own Son who died for her, was alive and real! He was with her always! He was here *now*. She was not alone, nor ever would be again.

She sat at the table not heeding the rising storm or the smoky furnace. For the first time in her life that she could remember she felt entirely rid of fear. There had been times when she had forgotten it because someone was caring for her and she was hiding behind one braver than herself. But always, when she remembered, the fear was there waiting to pounce on her when she was alone. And always she would run to shelter in another's strength.

At first there had been her mother. One of the few memories of her early childhood was of seeking comfort in Mommy's arms and bed. At the thought of this came that old familiar feeling of almost remembering what it was she feared. Only now it didn't bother her as it used to. For without remembering it she had conquered it.

"By the sword of the Spirit, the Word of God," she whispered.

After her mother had left her there had been Nona. What a burden she must have been to Nona! Through all those long years at the Home and the ones when they had lived together in the city Nona had shielded and strengthened her at the expense of her own strength.

Then, when Nona fell in the battle, Dave had come. He had been so gentle and understanding that she had rested completely in his love and care. Even when he was physically helpless it was his courage that upheld her. And in those months when he was discouraged and she had to keep cheerful it was his need that had upheld her.

Amy Moxon, too, had borne her share of JoAnne's weakness. And Martha and John, in their unselfish ways, had put themselves between her and her fears. Even Davie's need of her with Dave away she had used to stimulate her small strength.

But now,— her heart felt a thrill of joy as she realized it — she didn't need any of them any more. She didn't even have to try to be brave. She need not pretend a strength she did not possess. She had found the Source of all strength, and when she felt weakest she would rest completely in Him. He was hers, and He had promised to be with her always. The dingy little kitchen took on a glory as the truth shone in her soul. He was here now!

Chapter 33

A SHRIEK from the other side of the house startled JoAnne from her reverie,— then another shriek, then a Babel of sounds, all frightened and hysterical. She hesitated to try to help, for surely Martha or John would be equal to any need. But as she stood the door burst open, and Mary, ashenfaced and sobbing, ran to her.

"Mis' JoAnne, Samjones has cut hisself all to pieces, an' mammy an' daddy's gone an' I'm scared. The blood is just spoutin'!"

She was right. When JoAnne entered Martha's kitchen and pushed aside the frightened children that clamored about her, she saw Samjones huddled in a chair, holding one hand wrapped in a towel which was rapidly becoming soaked with bright red, and staring at her with piteous, frightened eyes. The emergency was great and she had no time to hesitate. She rushed to her own room for some bandages, then back to the kitchen.

"Mary, help me here. We have to get a bandage on. You hold this while I see what —"

She broke off and hastily grabbed the bandage as she

saw the spurting red blood from the slash in Samjones' wrist.

"I'll have to put on a tourniquet," she gasped. "Mary, call the doctor and tell him to — No! call the hospital and ask them to send someone at once. It's Central 3-4300. Tell them to come quickly!"

Mary ran to the telephone while JoAnne enlisted little Ann's aid.

"Here, Ann, hold this bandage and don't let it loosen while I — no,— hold it tighter! Oh no! I'll have to hold it. You get me a pencil or a spoon or *anything* I can twist in this bandage!"

She held the bandaged arm, her finger feeling desperately for the artery, and was relieved at last to see the bleeding stop. Then when Ann came with a spoon she thrust the handle under the bandage and twisted it. Cautiously withdrawing her finger she noted with satisfaction that the tourniquet seemed to be effective.

"So much for first aid lessons at the Home," she thought.

Her relief was short-lived, for Mary came back crying, "I can't get them, Mis' JoAnne," she sobbed. "Central won't answer. The telephone is jus' *dead*."

"Then try ours."

"I did. It's dead, too. There's a big tree down across the street and I guess the wires are broken."

"Well, where's Lute and Jud? They'll have to go to the hospital for help."

"They not here. They went to Scouts an'—"

"Then you'll have to go,— you and Ann. No, don't cry. You'll *have* to, Mary, or Samjones will die!"

Mary, whimpering, went for her coat. JoAnne, turning back to the little boy, realized that by the time the little girls traveled eight blocks to the hospital it would be too late. Samjones had slid off the low chair and was lying in an unconscious heap on the floor. The red stain on the bandage was spreading again. If his life were to be saved she must have help long before the return trip could be made.

"What will I do? Oh, dear Father, help us!"

Then to her needy soul came a Voice, the Voice that had lifted her from the depths a short half hour ago.

"I am with thee alway!"

"Mary!" she called. "Don't get your wraps. You and Ann go to the basement and get that old buggy of Cissy's. It will be better than Davie's cart. I am going to take Samjones to the hospital."

While the girls struggled she tightened the bandages, wrapped the little boy in a warm blanket, and hurried into her raincoat and hood. Only then did she remember her own sick child. But she did not falter though she whispered through trembling lips,

"Please, God, take care of Davie and don't let his croup come back when I'm not here!"

She placed the unconscious boy in the buggy and covered it with Martha's plastic tablecloth to keep out the rain.

"Listen, Mary. If your daddy comes tell him where I've gone and tell him to follow me. I'm going to take the shortcut through the viaduct."

"You mustn't! You'll have to cross all the tracks an'—"

"I know it, but that's the only way I can get there in time. You will watch Davie, won't you, Mary? If he wakes up give him one of those pink tablets on my dresser. And if he coughs give him a teaspoonful of the brown syrup beside the clock. And — you and Ann can pray, can't you?"

The tearful little girls promised, and she started out into the storm. It had been increasing in violence all evening and she felt the full force of it as she turned into the alley. Fortunately the wind was at her back. She could not have faced it and pushed the heavy buggy. She should have worn boots, for the water flowed like a river down the middle of the alley. But it was too late to think of that now. The wind whipped and tore at her and blew her along so fast that she stumbled and almost fell several times. Samjones aroused and started to cry, and she had to quiet him with all the sternness she could command.

At the end of the block, where the railroad embankment made a dead end to the streets of the neighborhood, there was a narrow viaduct which had been cut through the embankment for the convenience of the workers in the railroad switching yards beyond. It was forbidden ground to anyone except those workers, but occasionally the men and older boys would use it as a short cut to the business district beyond the tracks,— the district where the hospital was located. It was this short cut that JoAnne proposed to use now.

The wind shrieked, the lightning flashed, and the thunder was so continuous that she thought it was the noise of trains. The water was running down over her face so that she could hardly see.

"It won't be raining in the viaduct," she thought. "And maybe the wind won't be so strong in there. I wish this buggy were a boat. That's what I need tonight."

She struggled on and after what seemed an hour, but which she knew was only minutes she reached the viaduct and breathed a sigh of relief.

"When I get in the shelter I'll stop for a minute's rest."

She started down the slope that led under the tracks, then drew back with a gasp of dismay. The weak light from the one bulb in the roof showed an expanse of swirling water. The sewer that led from the viaduct had reversed, and instead of draining it, was pouring water in from some flooded higher level. Cautiously she advanced testing the depth carefully as she went.

"I know there aren't any sudden drops so I should be able to go along. If it gets too deep I may have to leave the buggy and carry him."

She pushed laboriously against the heavy buggy, and realized that she would never dare abandon it, for without its weight she might be swept from her feet. Deeper and deeper they went.

"I'm glad I have this high old buggy. Davie's cart would have been submerged by this time. The light must be about in the middle. It ought to get more shallow soon.

The water was rising however, as fast as she was progressing, and it was only when she reached the end and the ascent began that they gained on it. Then she faced a new difficulty. Try as she would she could not push the buggy up the slope made slick by the muddy water that had washed down.

"Oh, I should have come by the other way. I don't dare go back for the water is getting deeper all the time. I'll have to go on and leave the buggy. It's only a block more. I'll carry him."

She lifted the table cover and poured the water off it. She felt for the bandages and found them wet and sticky. How much of it was blood and how much water she could not tell.

"Samjones, are you awake?"

"Ye — s," came a weak whimper.

"If I pick you up can you hold onto me with the arm that wasn't cut?"

"I — I — try."

She wrapped him in the table cover, lifted him on one arm and felt him clutch her frantically. With the free hand she felt her way along the wall. The light was now at her back, and she felt as if she were facing a black abyss. The ground was rising however, and step by step she went with it. By her side the Voice whispered, "I am with you alway."

She reached the level path, and in the distance she could see the lighted windows of the hospital. But between her and it stretched a block crisscrossed with tracks and lighted by confusing red and green lights that shone weakly through the driving rain and only served to confuse her.

"I know I'm on the path now," she thought. "I'll let the lightning take care of me. I won't watch those other lights. I'll keep my eyes on the path and when there's a flash I'll go as far as I can see and wait for another. They're almost constant."

She had both arms around the boy now, and she realized he would be an almost impossible burden before she reached help.

"The Lord he it is that goeth before thee. He will not leave thee nor forsake thee."

"Yes, I know it, Lord, and I do thank You. I can't do this alone, but I can follow if You will lead."

At the hospital a young interne was talking to the nurse at the receiving desk when a noise at the door made them turn. Someone fumbled at the latch, partially opened the door, then let it shut again as a gust of wind caught it.

"Someone's trying to get in," the doctor exclaimed, running across the hall. The nurse was at his side as he opened the door.

"Get a chair," he said, stooping to the figure that was struggling to its feet. He lifted them both, JoAnne and Samjones, and carried them inside where the nurse met them.

"Oh, don't mind me!" JoAnne cried. "It's the little boy. I think he's bleeding to death."

The interne set her down and reached for the boy. Unwrapping the cover he took one look and started running for the emergency room.

The nurse turned to JoAnne. "Aren't you Mrs. Robertson? I took care of your husband when he was here several years ago. Who brought you in?"

"I brought—both of us. I'm all right,—but I couldn't

open the door. That's Martha's boy,— Martha Moseby. She's here now — I think she's on five east. I just — want to —" She swayed with weakness and the nurse helped her to a chair.

Another nurse came with a hot drink.

"They're working on the boy now, and the doctor said for you to have this and then take off your wet shoes and lie down. I'll get you a pair of my slippers while yours dry."

She was too tired to object, and in the warmth of the heavy blanket on the couch she fell asleep.

When she awakened it was to find Martha standing over her with her brown eyes full of tears.

"You save' my boy's life, JoAnne," she said chokingly. "He's all fix' up now an' had a transfusion. Now I know you wan' a go home to Davie. I hope he ain' miss you. Jawn an' the boys got home an' Jawn come right here. Lute an' Jud's takin' care of things. Dr. Crews say he'll take you home."

As JoAnne struggled to her feet and reached for her shoes Martha spoke again. "That Samjones! I tol' him not to whittle with my carvin' knife. I'll *tan* him! He's sleepin' now, bless his heart! An' I'll thank you an' the good Lord always when I look at him. You saved him,— an' you so little an' scared."

"I'm not afraid any more." JoAnne laughed shakily. "I've found a cure, Martha. And He'll never leave me. He promised."

Martha's face lighted as she caught JoAnne's meaning. "He sure won't, an' He's all you need."

She went off down the hall, but as they were leaving

she came running back. "I clean forgot. Miss Melton called awhile ago. She say she can't get the house. She goin'a stay all night at her sister's an' wants we should shut her window. Will you do it?"

Chapter 34

THE RAIN AND WIND were still furiously whirling about them as the doctor's car wound its way between the tree branches that littered the streets. But JoAnne hardly heard it. All she cared about was that soon she could crawl into bed beside Davie and go to sleep. As the doctor turned to leave after taking her to the door he said in embarrassed admiration,

"Martha's husband told us just how you got to the hospital tonight. I'd — I'd like to shake your hand. Will you tell that husband of yours that we all decided tonight that you are really quite a big little girl?"

She found Lute and Jud and Mary waiting anxiously in her living room. After she had reassured them she sent them home and turned thankfully to the bedroom where Davie slept soundly.

"Only one o'clock!" she said, glancing at the little alarm clock on the dresser. "It seems like a week ago that I sat at the kitchen table and 'got a glory,' as Martha would say. It really was a glory, too. In spite of the blood and thunder and wind and rain, I wasn't frightened any worse than *anyone* would be to think a child might die in his arms. I really think I'm cured. I'll never be brave but I don't have to be. I have One who is brave and that's all I need."

She turned down the blankets on her bed, thinking as she did so, "How soft and snug they look. I hope Davie lets me sleep until ten in the morning. But he won't."

A fresh burst of rain struck the windows and she remembered Martha's last admonition. Miss Melton's window must be shut.

"Probably the room is completely soaked by now, but I'd better see anyway."

She had never visited Miss Melton in her attic room, but it was the only one on the third floor so there could be no mistake. As she climbed the stairs after passing the second floor where the Katz and Polowsky apartments were dark and quiet, the creaking of the steps sounded loudly in the silence. Again that sense of the familiar came fleetingly to her. Sometime she must have climbed just such a stairway as this. The low light in the hall was enough to light Miss Melton's room, and she hurried across the floor in the half dark to the window. It was already closed, and the dry sill testified that it had not been open tonight. As she turned to leave her eye caught sight of a lighted sign that flared across the eastern sky and shone brightly in spite of the rain. Then she knew! Through the rain that sign appeared much as it must have looked to a near-sighted child — hazy and indistinct. This was the room she and her mother had lived in at one time. She had stood at this window and gazed at this sign. To make the assurance doubly sure she turned to the west. There stood the three smoke stacks that looked like three steps down from the sky. And across the upper half of the window stretched a branch of the big tree by the corner of the house. Her heart was beating quickly as she hurried across the floor and pushed the light switch by the door. The sense of familiarity vanished for this cozy, dainty apartment bore no resemblance to the plain one she remembered. But it was the same. She noted the corner closet, the sloping ceiling. She remembered those. And when she turned again to the window she was reassured. As she went down the two flights of stairs the wonder of it stayed with her, and as she passed the closed front door she saw it as a four-year-old saw it when going out for occasional trips with her mother.

Back in her own apartment she thought it all out. The outer appearance of the neighborhood had been changed since the street had been filled in. Anyway, she had probably seldom seen it. As a child she had never been in these rooms. If it were true, if she was not dreaming up the fantastic situation, then John's studio across the hall must be the room where some woman used to scold her as she sat, a terrified, lonely girl, in the corner behind the other bolder little ones. She could not remember how the woman looked except that she was big and cross and used to — ! JoAnne's breath caught sharply. If this really was the same place, if she had lived here in those baby years, then down in the basement was the thing that had been terror to her for over twenty years. She did not know what it was. Only tonight was the illusive memory becoming something she could get hold of. She only remembered being jerked down some stairs and being alone with IT. What could it have been? Her memory could not pierce the wall of the years.

She knew what she must do. She must go down into that basement and dispel forever her fear. Whatever was there must be met and faced. She did not like the idea of going alone on this gloomy night, but it had to be done, and perhaps it was best this way.

Taking the flashlight from her dresser she tiptoed past Davie's crib and into the kitchen. The Bible still lay on the table, open at the last reference she had found. The sight of it brought a swift sense of safety.

"Lo, I am with you alway."

The steps to the basement led down from the back entry. JoAnne pushed the switch at the head of the stairs and saw the room below light up. She went down cautiously, looking carefully to see if anything might come into view that would answer the riddle. But it seemed only an ordinary basement, a coal bin at one side, a balky furnace in the middle, and the usual collection of clutter against the walls. The low wattage bulb that hung by a cord from the ceiling cast a dim light over it all.

She circled the room warily, feeling certain that some place in this cellar lay the secret of her lifelong fears. A pile of orange crates and other bits of wood that Lute and Jud had gathered for kindling leaned against the steps at one side. Peering behind this pile JoAnne saw a small door which seemed to belong to an under-stair closet. She felt a return of the coldness that used to presage a spell of hysterics, but she did not hesitate. This was her goal. She knew it. So she pulled the boxes aside and turned the wooden button which held the door shut.

"I am with you alway."

She drew a long breath, stepped to the door and pushed the button of the flashlight. It was a small enclosure, roofed by the wooden steps, four feet high at one end, and sloping to about eight inches at the other. The floor was cluttered with paper and rags and old trash of all sorts. Apparently this was one place that Martha's genius for order and cleanliness had not yet reached.

Against the outer wall, six inches or so from the floor, a concrete ledge had been built. It was only about eight inches wide, and as JoAnne gazed at it her eyes grew misty at the recollection of a tiny frightened girl climbing frantically onto that ledge and clinging there in terror as the footsteps that had accompanied her down receded up the stairs. The real time spent thus could not have been long, but as she looked back on it now it appeared to fill most of her days. She could remember the panic and the determination not to get down on the floor. What could have been the cause? What could have brought her to such extremity of fear?

A rustling in the papers at her feet made her start, and she stepped quickly aside as a frightened mouse scurried across the floor. At last the picture was complete! She knew what the baby had feared.

"Poor little tot," she whispered. "Shut in here just because she was clumsy and slow. Poor, half-blind baby! I don't blame her for being terrified. I don't like mice even now."

She fastened the door again and went back up the

stairs. As she turned out the basement light and closed the door she thought with a flash of triumph, "I've met it and I've licked it! The Lord was with me, just like He said."

When she went to tuck Davie's covers more securely about him he was lying so relaxed and quiet that she knew there would be no croup tonight.

"You precious!" she whispered. "We'll both sleep better tonight. — Oh, God, help me to teach him early how to meet and defeat fear. Keep both my Daves safe and bring us together again."

Chapter 35

THE SIX MONTHS Mr. Brantwell had mentioned had passed, yet there was no hint of plans for return in Dave's letters. JoAnne tried to be patient, but as day followed day and they became weeks, four of which would turn into another month, she was beset with doubt. Against her own better judgment she wrote to him asking him to tell her frankly what they could expect. Had something gone wrong, and were they keeping the discouraging news away from her?

Dave's answer was prompt. "No, keeda, we're not shielding you from disappointment. I am coming out on top eventually. But it's a tough grind and I can't hurry it up. I did not realize how soft I had grown and how much building up there was to do. I am going to come up to Dad's and your expectations for me if it takes a year to do it. I did plan on being home for Thanksgiving, but I realize I can't make it. I am gaining every day, however, and the very first moment the doctor says so I'll be heading for home. Don't let Davie forget his dad."

JoAnne busied herself with the task at hand, trying to work so hard each day that night would bring unbroken sleep. The day before Thanksgiving Amy Moxon came with her car and carried them off for a happy four days on a farm two hundred miles from the city. It was JoAnne's first experience of Thanksgiving in a large family, and it made her acutely nostalgic for the things that might have been but never would be. She renewed in her mind, however, the determination to start planning for their own home as soon as Dave got back to work. The dream home had changed its dimensions and location since the days of the long rides through country lanes, but it was still there and they would make it come true.

Now she set Christmas as the time for Dave to come home. She did not mention it to Dave, or even to Mr. Brantwell or Amy. But she told Martha one night when that good neighbor came to the door with a plate of fresh cookies and found her making popcorn strings. Noting Martha's look of astonishment she explained.

"I *know* Dave is going to be home for Christmas. He always wants popcorn balls and strings on the tree because that's the way his mother had it."

"Do you hones' think he'll be home for Christmas?"

"Well, I'm hoping so hard and praying so hard that I am sure it will be that way. It will be the first Christmas that Davie will be able to understand what's going on, and I do *so* want Dave here." Her voice broke. "Won't you pray with me, Martha? "

"I sure will, honey, an' I get Jawn to pray, too. I reckon he got a lot more influence with God than I have."

"I don't think so," said JoAnne stoutly. "You come

242

as near to fulfilling all the requirements for answered prayer as anyone I know of. It will give me a big boost if I know that both of you are praying."

"Oh, we all pray. Clean down to Samjones and Cissy. An' if they's anythin' I can do to he'p you get your trimmin's made an' your bakin' done, let me know."

Amy and Mr. Brantwell looked askance at these preparations.

"You might be building up for a tumble," Amy cautioned.

"I don't care," said JoAnne. "It can't hurt to be ready, and I think he'll be home by then."

In mid-December Mr. Brantwell could stand it no longer. Someone had to make a trip to the Los Angeles store. He'd do it himself and go past the sanitarium. By flying both ways he could transact his business, visit Dave, and be back in a week.

"I'll bring a first hand report, little lady," he promised. "And if there's anything on earth that will hasten the boy's return I'll do my best to find it. And I'll let you know as soon as I get home. I might even call you from the sanitarium."

But the week passed and he did not call. The decorations were finished and waiting in boxes on the table. She had hoped Dave would be able to trim the lower boughs of the small tree she had planned. Several canisters on the kitchen shelf were filled with Christmas cookies, and a fruit cake — the first she had ever made — was ripening in its box. There was nothing left for her to do, and because the store was so busy with Christmas selling the office work was allowed to fall behind so there was less than usual sent out to her.

With so much time on her hands and with her mind unoccupied with regular work it was easy for her to fall into a mood of doubt. She became convinced again that disappointment lay ahead of them. Else why had Mr. Brantwell neither called nor written? Dave's letters were merely repetitions of what he had said many times before and ceased to bring conviction to her. Martha sensed her mood, for the sight of the little figure going to and fro to the market or mail box bespoke despondency. Having noted it, Martha had to do something about it.

JoAnne was trying to fix Davie's automobile and thinking how much more efficiently Dave could have done it, when a knock sounded at the door, then it was pushed open just enough to allow Martha's bulky form to be seen.

"If you busy I come some other time."

"No, indeed. Can I do something for you?"

"Yes. I gotta lead a devotional at my group meetin' tomorrow night. I know what I wanta say, an' I hunted up a lot o' verses I wanta use but I can't string 'em together right. I don' have any time today cause I'm workin' overtime at the hospital, an' I'm wonderin' could you he'p me?"

"I'd be mighty glad to try. You're always doing something for me and I don't have much chance to help you."

For two hours she worked diligently on the devotional, taking Martha's Scripture findings and weaving them into an orderly and well-worded presentation. She did not know that Martha had discarded an almost prepared lesson that she might bring these particular verses to JoAnne's attention. But as she studied and wrote, the message she was preparing began to make its impact on her heart. How weak she was, and how quick to forget the things God was teaching her! She had been triumphantly conscious of God's continual help and presence in her physical needs, but she was failing to realize His constant care and concern for her spiritual requirements. He would prove Himself sufficient for all the future and would supply grace to enable her to meet any circumstance He would send.

"I will trust and I *will* rejoice," she whispered that evening as she stood at the window and watched the snowflakes sifting down on the street outside. If this kept up they would have a white Christmas. "Oh, God, please let Dave come home to us by then. But more than anything else, I want You to keep me trusting and rejoicing. Whatever the future holds, I know You are in it and we in Thee. So I'm not afraid."

A car was stopping in front of the house. The light from the corner shone dimly through the snow and she did not realize that it belonged to Mr. Brantwell until she saw the driver get out and assist the old man and Amy Moxon from the back seat. They all started down the steps that led from the sidewalk. Were they bringing bad news, that Amy had come with him? Thankful for Mr. Brantwell's slowness she ran into the bedroom taking off her faded housecoat as she went. She had buttoned a fresh dress and brushed her hair before she heard them on the porch. She closed the kitchen door to hide the lines of laundry that stretched across it, then turned to face whatever might come. As she turned, the door opened and they faced her.

Her face whitened and her eyes grew wide and dark. Mr. Brantwell's face was shining and his eyes glowing, but JoAnne did not see him. For beside him, tall and straight, brown from the sun of the south and with hair sprinkled with the snow of the north, stood Dave! She backed against the kitchen door and stood there with arms spread at her sides as if afraid to move. Davie, who had been aroused by her rush into the bedroom, had climbed out of his bed and stood wonderingly in the doorway. For a long minute no one spoke. Then Dave's voice, laughing and excited, broke the silence.

"Will you forgive me for fooling you, honey? For a long time I didn't dare tell you for fear it wouldn't last. Then when I found it was true, I wanted to come and tell you myself."

Still she stared until he started toward her. Then with a rush she was in his arms. Mr. Brantwell turned to where John and Martha and Amy Moxon were watching from the studio door.

"If you folks don't mind," he said shakily, "I'd like to sit down awhile." So they turned away and Amy closed the door.

Back in the little apartment JoAnne lifted a radiant face to Dave and said tremulously, "I — I — can't believe it, Dave."

"Neither can I, but it's true. It's been a hard pull, honey, but I won out. I can't run any races yet, but I can walk, and by spring I'll race you on the beach in the sunrise!"

Davie was tugging at JoAnne's skirt, and Dave stooped to lift him. "It's your old pal come back, fella. Do you know me?"

The little boy looked long at the man, then his eyes went to the picture on the table, then back again. In a whisper he ventured the word that Dave wanted to hear. "Daddy!" Dave held him closely as if trying to satisfy eight months of hunger. Then he said huskily,

"I wonder if Mommy would get us a blanket so you could stay up for awhile."

She brought the blanket and they all sat together on the davenport, Dave with one arm holding Davie and the other encircling JoAnne. She was shaking from excitement, and Dave said contritely,

"I didn't mean to frighten you, darling. I guess it was a shock."

"I'll be all right. So much happiness at once made me feel weak. Tell me how it happened."

He held her close and began to talk, knowing that his presence and his voice would calm her.

"Do you remember my famous catch in the ball game in August? Well, that started it. You see I *jumped* and caught that ball! It all happened so quickly that no one could tell how I did it. But I did. I not only jumped, but I took two steps. Of course I fell ignominiously in the dirt, but I had the ball. Then the doctors took charge of me and put me through the stiffest course I ever met. They said I could walk if I wanted to badly enough. And all the time I was wanting to so badly I could have cried. But I guess I did believe them a bit. You see, I had jumped once here at home. I wouldn't let them

247

tell you for I thought it would never happen again. But after that second time I began to hope. And did I *work*? And they worked. They rubbed and shocked me. They encouraged me and bullied me. It was awful. They just kept telling me I could do it, and one morning in September I did. I had to be helped a lot at first, for these beautiful feet were pretty clumsy. But as soon as I knew I could I was willing to work day and night. They had to make me go to bed. I even got up once in the middle of the night and tried it out to see if it was true or if I had been dreaming. It was a king-size job, but it was worth it!"

He stopped to tuck the cover more closely about Davie and to smile down into the little upturned face that was studying him. JoAnne, grown quiet, noticed with a new awareness how much they looked alike, these two Daves.

"At first I wouldn't let myself hope too much. I kept expecting to have those legs go dead again. But the doctors said that I would be O.K. and that it was permanent. I sailed from there on out! A few weeks ago they let me try to drive and last week I got a license. The day Dad came I went to the station with the driver to meet the plane. We didn't know who was coming. When Dad saw me he almost fainted, and I felt rather shaky at the unexpected meeting. The next day I took him for a drive. So they turned me loose and let me come home with him. I drove here and Harry is waiting out there in the car to take Dad home. I think he wanted Amy with us when we came for fear you'd go clear out when you saw me. But I wasn't afraid. I knew my gal well enough to know that if sorrow and trouble couldn't knock her down, joy wouldn't."

"It didn't, even though I didn't know life could hold such joy."

Davie had fallen asleep, and together they tucked him into bed. Dave looked long at him as he lay in childish relaxation.

"I've thought of you two every night when you'd be putting him to bed. I knew you'd be praying by his side. Can't we do it now?"

So they prayed, thanking God for His great gifts to them, and asking His blessing on their boy.

Back in the living room Dave pulled JoAnne down beside him again.

"We've heard all about me. Now Mrs. Robertson will report."

"On what? I've written every day."

"But you kept something back from me also. I'm not the only one that could spring a surprise."

"What do you mean?"

"Dad told me about your taking Samjones to the hospital. He dwelt most on the fact that you were a very small girl to carry a five-year-old boy. But that didn't surprise me. I know you are strong physically. But there was one thing Dad said that I couldn't forget. I've been thinking about it ever since. It means that something big has happened to you. He said it was the night of the big storm in October. We read about that storm in the papers and I wondered how you took it, with you and Davie alone in the apartment. I knew you'd been a pretty brave girl ever since you showed me how to find the spring in the valley. And when it thundered you didn't scream. But you *did* tremble. And no frightened child carried that big boy through that flooded viaduct and across those tracks in the middle of the worst storm this city has seen in ten years. For some reason you weren't frightened. Tell me about it."

"Well—it's a long story. Isn't it queer how you can know a verse of Scripture all your life, can even quote it to other people, and yet never comprehend it the least bit? I think I memorized the last few verses in Matthew when I was in the primary department. And I thought of course I understood them. You know better than anyone ever has just how great a coward I've always been. All my life I've drawn strength from others. You all thought I had overcome it when you were so much in need of me. But I hadn't really. I was just forced by your need to brace you up. I thought I was real brave. But I wasn't a bit. Even though you were ill I was leaning on you. I found out when you left that the peace and joy I had were all dependent on someone else. Why, I even used to hang onto Davie's hand when I went to bed, to get what strength I could from him."

His arm tightened across her shoulders as if it were hard for him to listen to the recital of her loneliness.

"In October it was so gloomy that I got a real spell of the dumps. I got to thinking that you might not come back, and that something might happen to Davie, and the hysterics were right around the corner. Your Bible was lying there, and I found a slip of paper on which you'd written some references. I read them all because you had written them and it made me seem closer to you. When

250

I came to the last one, 'Lo, I am with you alway,' it suddenly came to me with a great burst of joy that it was *true!* I could quit trying to be brave and strong and I could just let Him take care of me all the time. You've been wonderful, Dave, but you did have to leave. And Nona did, and my mother. Even when you're here you can't stay with me every minute, and there could be dangers that you weren't equal to. But Christ has promised to be with me all the time, and nothing is too hard for Him. I don't even have to think about the things I don't like. It was while I was sitting there and rejoicing in all this that Mary came for me. Martha and Jawn were both gone, and so were Lute and Jud. I had to do something. There wasn't time to go around so I went through the viaduct and across the tracks. That's all. I wasn't afraid because I wasn't alone."

He looked at her and smiled. Then he shook his head.

"So that's all. It's as simple as that. A lifelong bugbear disappears into outer darkness. And you never even found out what it was."

"Oh, yes, I did. That very night I met and conquered the cause of the whole thing. It didn't get the headlines but to me it was as big a thing as the trip to the hospital."

She told him of her recognition of the house and of her trip down into the basement to lay forever the ghost of the past. He laughed once at the realization that it was a mouse that she had feared in those baby days, but his face sobered and his eyes grew misty at the picture of the panic-stricken little girl, and at his knowledge of the cost she had paid for almost twenty-five years for the cruelty of the woman who had so punished her.

"Oh, I've felt like a new person ever since. It makes me ashamed that, with all my talk of the new life in Christ, I was so slow taking it as a reality in myself. But it *is* real now. Do you know what I feel like tonight?"

"I'd like to know."

"I feel like I do when I look at the sunrise. Life gets brighter and brighter all the time."

He stood up, drawing her with him. Out of doors the snow fell silently, covering the ugliness and sordidness of the shabby street. The light on the corner shining through the falling flakes made a rainbow-colored nimbus against the background of the dark sky.

"It doesn't take a sunrise or even a real rainbow to show God's glory, does it, keeda? He can make a rainbow out of a street lamp — or a giant out of a little bit of a girl!"

THE END

THEN AM I STRONG

Francena H. Arnold

Then Am I Strong recounts the challenges and problems of a near sighted orphan, JoAnne, who struggles under a constant terrifying fear of darkness and loneliness.

Throughout her childhood and young adult years she is dependent upon Nona, a close friend. Nona leaves, and JoAnne's dependence shifts to another friend —Dave. Love for Dave soon supplants the friendship of Nona, but JoAnne's insecurities still keep her very immature. She marries Dave for better or for worse. Unfortunately the worst comes. With their many complications and problems comes an increasing knowledge of what Christ meant when He said, "Lo I am with you always."

After a stormy night of trial comes a glorious sunrise which routs the dark fears of this newly established home. A story of encouragement and true hope.

0195N8P